Women Lie Men Lie Part 4

A. Roy Milligan

Previous in Women Lie Men Lie Part 3:

At around 3 a.m., Linda woke JC up by sucking his dick. He thought he was dreaming at first until he opened his eyes and saw her mouth sliding down his pole. After he came, she got up and took another shower.

JC fell asleep waiting for her to come out and when he awoke, she was putting her coat on. He got up to leave as well when she said, "No, relax. There's a spare key, the alarm code and your money on the dresser. Go to sleep and leave whenever you want to. I'll be back in three days. Come and go as you will. My daughter will be here, I let her know you'd be staying."

"You sure Linda? Your daughter doesn't know me. I don't want her to freak out and call the police."

"It's fine, I trust you. It's not a problem." Linda gave him a big kiss, gave his dick one last lick, and left in a hurry before she convinced herself to stay longer and be late for her plane. JC was shocked by her hospitality, they had just met, yet she was trusting him with her most prized possessions, including her fine ass daughter. He fell back to sleep and was awakened about an hour with a knock on the bedroom door. "Who is it?" he asked, pulling the sheet over his naked body. "Me, Sandra. Can I come in?"

Chapter 1

JC jumped up to sit on the bed, jerking wide awake from his sleep with sweat forming a thick sheen all over his body. He was completely drenched from the neck down, small beads of sweat rolling off his chest were dampering the sheets beneath him. "Oh shit!" he shouted loudly, waking Sandra who was fast asleep next to him. She nearly fell off the bed before she caught herself in the nick of time.

"Oh my God. What's wrong!" she yelled, looking at the sweat all over his face. He was sweating like he had just ran a marathon and panting almost as hard. He looked around as if he had seen a ghost. The terrified look he had on his face scared the shit out of her, but all she could ask was, "What's wrong? Talk to me JC, you're scaring me." She looked around her mom's room, searching desperately for some kind of clue, but came up with nothing. "Did you just have a bad dream?" she asked as she moved closer to him, putting her arm on his to try to calm him down. His chest was rising high and falling low at a quick speed as he was breathing heavily.

"Damn," he murmured as he took in a deep breath to try to calm himself and then shook his head. "What the fuck was that? I just had the worst dream ever. What time is it?" Although he asked for the time, what he really wanted to ask was what day it was. His dream seemed so real he was

1

confused about reality and what was going on in his life. He started wondering if this was a sign of some sort. Was God trying to relay a message to him? He reached up and felt his face, running his palms and still-shaking fingers over it and looked down at his naked body. Everything was drenched.

"It's 8:48. Calm down. Everything is ok. It's just me and you here," Sandra said soothingly, although her voice was tinged with anxious concern. "You been scaring me since we went to sleep. I thought about going to my room, but I'm glad I didn't. First you was talking in your sleep, then jumping non-stop. You might want to go to a sleep specialist and see what's going on." She paused and looked him over, her gaze sweeping over his sweat-drenched body. "Look how sweaty you are. That had to be a crazy dream for you to be sweating like that and you been sitting right there all night not even moving, just jumping."

JC nodded in agreement, wiping a droplet of sweat that rolled down his forehead to sting his eye. "It was crazy as hell. I don't know how I'm this sweaty neither. That shit seemed so damn real." He sat up on the bed with his back against the headboard, thinking about what had happened in his dream. He felt like he remembered most of it although some parts were starting to get a bit hazy.

"You mind talking about it? It seems like some serious shit man. I honestly never seen anyone sweat that much from a dream. It's not even that hot in here. You want some water or something?" Sandra sat next to him and studied him carefully, giving him space.

Chapter 2

JC thought about it for a second and figured he could tell her, just as long as he left the real names out of it. There was no harm in that. "So at the beginning, it was like, I was dealing with this white girl. She was my girlfriend I think. For some reason, I wanted to kill her for something she did to me. I don't know if she had cheated on me or what but I wanted to kill her. I went to her house and beat her half to death then I shot her. After that, a guy I use to deal with, I went to his sister house and his moms house. I killed them too."

"What the fuck?" Sandra exclaimed, her eyes going wide with shock as she was listening to JC. Everything he was saying sounded weird to her. She knew nothing about that life so she could hardly believe her ears.

"But wait..." JC interrupted, holding up his hand. "I think I had a girlfriend here in Atlanta. I'm serious as hell right now," he told her insistently, frowning a little to show her that he wasn't kidding. "This is really what happened. The shit was weird as fuck. Oh shit, you was in my dream too."

"Seriously? Did you kill me too, JC?" she asked sarcastically, rolling her eyes so hard they almost disappeared into her head.

JC laughed a little. "No I didn't kill you. You had called me and told me you was pregnant and I was telling you that I wasn't the father," he said. There was a pause where they looked at each other. Then they both started cracking up, laughing loudly together. "But hold on, there's more," he told her as she leaned in to listen to what he was about to say. "So the girlfriend that had the ex, I was on my way to meet up with her. I think she was at her mom's house or something. But when I got there, she was standing in the door way, like crying or something. I was sitting there wondering why the fuck she was crying so I'm like waving my hands to her for her to come out. She didn't, so I called her and she didn't answer. A couple seconds later, police cars came from every which way and surrounded me. I floored the car I was in and ran straight through her mom's garage and got out and ran after her inside the house. She ran out the front door but I chased her ass and shot her in her back twice and that's when the police shot me like 30 damn times. That shit seemed so fucking real, I have chills just telling you." He ran through all the details in a single breath, saying everything out loud as the details of the dream came to him in a mad rush, even details he couldn't remember at first.

Sandra had been listening intently and nodded. "Wow, yes that sounds very crazy. Dreaming about killing people and even being killed is crazy enough. I never had a dream like that before. I'm shaking, just listening to all of it." JC could tell that she was affected by his dream. She looked a little worried.

"Where's your mom at? She did go on a vacation right?" JC asked suddenly.

4

She giggled, throwing him an odd look. "Yes, that wasn't part of your dream. That was actually real. Are you staying here until she get back?"

"Um I don't know yet. I have to figure some shit out."

"Like?"

"Just life situations, nothing too serious. I just have a whole lot on my mind, that's all."

Chapter 3

With that, he got up off the bed and looked around to find his clothes. They were scattered all across the room. He found his boxers hanging off the back of a chair and started putting them on, still in deep thought.

"I can tell you have a lot on your mind. If it's anything I can do for you, other than what I did earlier, let me know," Sandra said as she smiled and winked at him, with a lascivious grin on her face. JC thought about all the things she had done before they went to sleep and grinned. Before he could think about reaching out to catch her, she slid out the bed and walked towards the door butt ass naked, her tits bouncing and her hips swinging as she went. Her little ass cheeks jiggled as he watched her leave, closing the door behind her.

Although that dream had shook JC, he now wanted to get focused. He looked around and realized he was inside of a really expensive mansion. Linda's bedroom was beautiful and plush, full of luxury furniture, and he was hoping she didn't have any cameras hidden away anywhere. The bedroom had floor to ceiling windows all on one side of the room that JC didn't even notice before. There was light streaming into the room through them, and he walked over to them to take a look outside. There were acres and acres of lush land with perfectly manicured lawns and hedges stretching far and wide and a big pool glistening clear blue below. He started to wonder if it was easy to get rich in Atlanta because everyone he was coming into contact with was doing really well for themselves.

JC walked around the room slowly, noticing all the expensive oak wood furniture, and he started imagining himself having something like this one day. This place had to have cost at least $8 million, he could tell from all the expensive details.

He walked back to the bed and grabbed his cell phone from the nightstand by the huge sized bed. He checked for missed calls and text messages, and he instantly thought about Jamie. Jamie was in his dream as well. He remembered Kelly tricked her into believing she was with a family member of his, and they were trying to surprise him for his birthday. Kelly was trying to find out his location. More and more of his dream was coming to him with every passing minute, but things still didn't make much sense. He did know he had to continue to lay low.

Chapter 4

"Sandra!" he yelled loud enough for his voice to carry through the walls, but no one responded. The place was so big, he just assumed there was no way she could have heard him so he got up and walked to the hallway. "Damn," he said as he saw tan marble floors stretching all the way down the hall. The walls were filled with expensive art work that probably cost thousands of dollars and a very expensive clock that was trimmed with gold. "Sandra!" he yelled again, a little louder this time, still staring at the art.

"Yes?" she shouted back, walking out of her room and into the hallway. She noticed JC staring at one of the paintings on the wall. She wasn't naked anymore since she had put on some black leggings and a bright orange sports bra.

"You know how to deactivate a Facebook page?" he asked her.

"Of course. It's pretty simple. I can help you out. Where's your phone?"

"Right here," JC went to the app and handed it to her. "What if I want to reactivate it?"

She leaned in and showed him what he supposed to go to. She was very good with technology, unlike JC. He wasn't bad but there was a lot he didn't understand. That's where Sandra and her tech skills came into the picture. "I heard Facebook gives away your location and shit. I don't like that. Is it a way I can somehow block that? I don't want people knowing where I'm at. That's some weird ass shit."

"I know, I wouldn't want everyone knowing where I am all the time either, that's some stalker ass shit. You can use a VPN. That's what I always use. I hate it when my location is revealed to people I don't even know. It usually don't give you the exact location, but still."

"What's A VPN? I never heard of that before."

"It stands for virtual private network. It basically gives you more security when you connect to the internet. Especially when you online shopping and using all your credit card info, bank info and all that stuff. You know what a IP address is right?"

"Yea, I've heard about a IP address, but never the VPN thing."

"So, a VPN is like putting a mask over a IP address. It makes you virtually untraceable. No one can pinpoint you. It encrypts your data once you go online. Like for example, I have plenty of friends that use a VPN when they go on the dark web. Some of them may be looking up some illegal stuff and don't want the government to know or anyone to know, so they use all kinds of things that can mask their info, like a VPN."

JC nodded. What Sandra was describing sounded like it was exactly what he needed. "Is a VPN free or it cost?"

"Yes it cost but it's really cheap," Sandra explained. "I think I pay like $15.00 a month or something. I can't remember but it's not expensive."

"How do I get one? I need that. Can I use yours? Like can we share?"

"The way it works, is I can add you on my account. I think I pay for 5 different devices but I'm only using two of them, so I can add you to one of those. All you have to do is download the Nord app and I'll give you my login information and show you what to do. It's very simple."

Chapter 5

She showed him how everything worked and it only took her about 20 minutes. Once she broke down how it worked, he felt safer. He had no clue he could make it look like he was in a whole different state or even country. With the VPN on his phone, he was sure nobody could track him.

As Sandra was playing with his phone, Juicy's name popped up on the screen. "Let me take this call," he said, quickly walking back into Linda's room and closing the door before picking up the call. "What's up baby?" he said smoothly, knowing she was going to be mad. He could even feel her anger coming in waves down through the phone although she hadn't even said a word to him yet.

"What's up? Where the fuck you at? I can't do this stupid shit with you JC. I'm not feeling this shit, none of this shit you doing. You a street nigga that loves to run the streets and I don't like it." She was pissed.

"Man, chillout. I told you I had some business to take care of. Where you at?"

"Where I been? I'm at my mom's. You know that," she retorted.

"Well I'll be there in a minute. I have a surprise for you. You over there tripping and you know I'm trying to get shit together for us."

She held the phone, not saying a word, but he knew she was wondering about the surprise he had for her. "What's the surprise, JC? You have another baby on the way?" she finally asked, sounding a little annoyed but also curious at the same time.

While he was on the phone, Sandra had come into the room with her finger on her lips, motioning for him to be quiet. She dropped to her knees on the carpet in front of him and was starting to pull down his boxers. JC tried to play it cool. He didn't want to give Juicy a reason to snap and hang up on him. He knew this was a bad idea but he wasn't about to turn down a blowjob. "Um, why would you say something like that? You have to wait and see what my surprise for you is. You gone like it though, although you over there trying to start a fight."

Seconds later, Sandra had his dick in her mouth and was sucking away, moving her head up and down just the way he liked it, flattening her tongue so that it was dragging along the sensitive underside of his dick. He wanted to sit down and enjoy her warm mouth but he knew he woulda for sure slipped up with Juicy if he got too relaxed so he kept standing, leaning against a wall to brace himself. Sandra thought it was funny for her to be sucking his dick while he was on the phone with another woman.

"We'll see. I'm not trying to start a fight with you. You staying away all night and not calling until the morning is where the fight started," Juicy told him, still sounding annoyed. "I'm mad right now so don't be trying to buy me stuff just to get back on my good side. And another thing that I'm highly irritated with you about is you wanting me to just sit in this house waiting on you to come back home or make things happen. That's not me at all. I don't like this and I've been thinking a lot."

Chapter 6

JC was standing there holding the phone, listening while he was making eye contact with Sandra. She was sucking him nice and slow while using both hands to stroke him, bobbing her head back and forth in smooth motions. She had his dick soaking wet as it went in and out her hot mouth. She kept looking up at him and grinning with his dick in her mouth, flicking her tongue over his tip to try to get him to react and lose control.

"I'm not sure how long I'm going to be able to sit still. I feel like I need to be out working until this baby really start showing. I'm missing thousands of dollars every night. I've been talking to some of my homegirls, and they been making plenty of money on regular nights. Me sitting here just waiting to see what you gone make happen, is not sitting right with me." She paused, then continued in a softer tone. "I'm not doubting you, I'm just saying, I can help too. I'm trying to be respectful towards you and believe everything going to be ok, but the more money we make, the better. Two is always better than one. I don't want to just sit at home all day, JC. I have nothing to do here. So, what you think about me hitting the clubs back up so I can make some money as well?" She waited for his answer silently on the other end of the line.

"I...I think, that's cool," he mumbled as he was nearly on his tippy toes, trying to keep his voice from sounding breathy and biting back the groans that threatened to emerge from his throat. Sandra had him nearly about to buss, but she stopped sucking his dick and started sucking on his balls instead.

"So you think I should get back out there before I start showing?" Juicy asked slowly, sounding hopeful.

Just then, Sandra sucked on his balls just right in a way that had him moaning, "Yesss baby."

Juicy giggled when she heard him, "Why you say it like that?"

"I'm just saying. Th- That don't...sound like a bad idea." He grabbed Sandra head and maneuvered it to make her go back to sucking his dick instead of licking his balls. He was trying to concentrate on the conversation with Juicy for a second. It was hard as hell with Sandra sucking his soul out of his damn dick.

Juicy sounded relieved when he said that. Her annoyed tone changed and it sounded like she was happy with his answer. "Thank you. I just felt like it only makes sense for both of us to be making money instead of just one of us. We a team and I want to help support as well. You know I get in the club and fuck it up. I'm mad about not having a good amount saved up, but it's gone be ok."

Chapter 7

"Baby... I agree." By now, he was cumming hard in Sandra's mouth, and she was swallowing it all down, gulp by gulp. "Thank you," he said with a deep satisfied sigh.

"Thanks for what?" Juicy asked, confused, not knowing he was talking to Sandra for the great head she had just given him.

He laughed a little as he was releasing his last drop into her mouth, milking it all out. "Just sharing your thoughts. But you are missing the point of why I said for you to do that."

"What's the point?" Juicy asked, letting out a small huff.

"All the shit that's been going on. All these killings and shit. I think it's just best not to be out like that until I find out what's going on." He paused as he thought for a moment before continuing in a firm tone that meant business. "The whole shit with Gloria and all that. That shit serious. I get you want to be out trying to help, but not in the damn strip club. You about to be my baby's mother. Why would I approve some shit like that?"

There was a moment of silence. It was clear she was trying to figure out what was going on. "You just was acting like it was ok a few minutes ago. What changed?"

JC started pulling up his boxers with his phone held between his shoulder and his ear. "I just wanted to hear you out and hear everything you had to say. We can talk more about it when I get there."

"Whatever, JC," she said, annoyed as she hung up in his face.

JC took a deep breath and grinned, tossing his phone aside and looking down at Sandra who was still on her knees in front of him wiping her mouth off on the back of her hand. She still had that saucy look in her eyes and he spoke down to her, trying to bite back a grin. "Damn that shit felt good as hell. You ain't about to keep getting this dick for free neither. What's wrong with you?"

She smiled and stood up, her hands on her hips as she arched her brow at him. "Are you serious, JC? I'm sure my mom paid you very well. I heard her on the phone bragging about you. Her and her friend Jamie was talking about how good your dick feels, which is the reason I wanted to see for myself. I had to try you out. I don't do this with all the guys she bring neither, so don't think that."

Chapter 8

"Yea, yea, yea. You keep running up on me, I'ma make your ass pay." At that, Sandra playfully swiped at him with her hand, and he grinned as he brushed it away. "Naw, I'm kidding. Just keep this between you and me. I ain't trying to mess up me and your mom business relationship just because she found out I'm fucking her daughter. She pay way too good so as long as you keep your mouth close, we good."

"Aww, don't worry about that," Sandra smiled. "I have plenty if you need something. You give me what I want, I give you what you want. You can have whatever you want. I will keep this between us for sure. I don't need my mom getting jealous of me fucking you better and sucking you better. The bitch still think she's 20. I don't want to have to fight her over you. At least, that's what happened once upon a time."

That piqued JC's interest, and he gave her a quizzical look. "What? You fought your mom over a guy?"

"Yes!" Sandra sighed. "She tried fucking my ex boyfriend when I wasn't around. She told him all these lies about different guys I had been with and had had over and all kinds of shit."

JC laughed loudly, "Damn she tripping. Well did it work? Did she fuck him?"

"Hell no. He didn't want her old ass. I had to slap that bitch a few times."

"Yea, we don't need any fighting going on. Keep this shit on the hush."

When Sandra left, JC hopped in the shower to wash off any remaining trace of her and then headed over to Juicy's mom's house. He had a nice amount of money on him and couldn't wait to show it to her. Juicy had been stressing because she hated living with her mom, and she didn't have the money to move at the moment. JC knew this would make her happy and make her feel a lot better.

Although things were looking good for him, he just couldn't seem to stop thinking about the dream he had. It seemed so real, and it kept replaying in his head over and over while he was driving. He thought about how everything was so unorganized in his life and how he needed to just get away for a while and get himself together. It was easier said than done though, with how things were now. His face was all over the news, and it wasn't safe for him to be in the streets so he was trying to figure something out fast. Even if he had to be an in house boyfriend for the moment, he was fine with that as long as he had him some money. That would smooth things over until he could figure out his next step.

Chapter 9

Taking a turn down the familiar road, he finally made it to Juicy's mom's house. When he pulled up, he parked in the driveway and sat in the car, pulling out his phone. He was about to call Juicy until he looked up and saw her standing in the doorway. At the sight of her, he instantly had a flash back about the dream he had. It was so vivid that he was frozen in place for a second as dozen of images flooded into his mind.

It didn't take too long before he snapped out of it and got out of his car. He walked inside to see Juicy waiting for him with a huge smile on her face. "Oh now you wanna look all cute and sexy after you was just going off on me over the phone," he told her with a grin, relieved to see that she wasn't in a bad mood like she had been when she was on the phone with him before.

She rolled her eyes affectionately and giggled, "Whatever, I missed you. I'm happy to see you." She moved in towards him, and hugged and kissed him on the lips. Then she stood back and looked at him expectantly. "So where's my surprise?"

"Where your mom go?" JC asked quickly, looking around the house.

"She gone. She'll be back later. She had to go to the grocery store and some more stuff she had on her little to do list paper. So we got time for a lil quickie. I need some dick bad." With a big smile, she started unbuckling his pants while simultaneously pulling him to the back room.

He laughed, letting himself be led away, "Oh really? You just gone take it, huh?" He followed her to the back room while holding the duffle bag he brought in.

"Lay down," she instructed, pushing him down on his back onto the bed and then climbing on top of him, her thighs straddling his hips as she started kissing him. He could tell she really wanted his dick bad right then. She then started easing out of her pajamas and thong, reaching down for his dick. When she wrapped her fingers around his length, she pouted, noticing he wasn't hard yet. She slid down and started sucking until it was good and hard, then she lined herself up with his dick and lowered herself down on it slowly and started riding him.

He gripped her ass cheeks while she continued to ride him, making herself cum after about 7 minutes.

"Roll over baby," he told her, as he got on top of her and slid his dick back inside her wet heat. He stood in a push up position and started dropping his dick firmly in and out of her.

"Shit!" she moaned as she pressed her hands on his stomach. "Oh God!" She kept moaning and gasping as he pounded his dick into her, faster and faster, smooth and deep. It wasn't long before her moans got to him.

"I'm about to cum," he groaned as he kept pumping until his body stiffened up and he was releasing is semen inside of her in a strong gush.

21

"Yes, give it all to me," she moaned as she rubbed his back and kissed his neck softly, her breath warming his skin.

Chapter 10

Minutes later once he'd milked all of his semen out into her, he got up and cleaned himself off. "So, you can gone ahead and pack your shit up." he told her casually, waiting for her reaction. "I got the money so we can move comfortably."

"Yayyy!" she screamed with delight, beaming at him. "I never unpacked."

He laughed and then started going through the bag and counting out the money. His fingers were shuffling through the crisp notes, his lips moving silently as he counted. Juicy didn't ask any questions, she was just happy to be able to do what she needed to do now that her problems were sorted. Ever since JC had came into her life, it was like everything got worse for her. She still loved him, but she couldn't understand why all this crazy stuff was happening around her.

"You been ready, huh?" he teased, fingering the notes and shuffling them in her direction.

Before she could answer, a series gun shots were ringing out, non-stop. He reacted out of pure instinct as Juicy was frozen in place with terror. "Get down!" JC yelled at her, grabbing her and dropping down to the floor. She resisted for a second because she was surprised and confused by what was going on, but he managed to drag her down to the ground with him.

"Oh my God, JC. What the fuck!" she shouted with her hand over her head, her eyes betraying her fear. The shots kept on firing, and they were both lying flat on the floor, careful to keep away from the windows. The bullets flew through the house, entering from the front. JC barley had time to think as the bullets rained around them. All he could do was stay as low as possible. He yanked on Juicy's arm to get her to follow him as he crawled on the ground on his belly out of the room. Looking up, he saw that the bullets had already hit the walls as they passed them. The only chance they had was to crawl as low as possible until they could get out of the house.

"JC, I'm scared. What the fuck is going on!" Juicy screamed over the pounding of the gun shots.

"Shut up, come on!" he yelled back at her, dragging her along with him and pulling her through the house. The gun shots were still going strong, the bullets littering the walls of the house with holes and destroying everything they hit. These guys had so much ammo, all JC could think of was Merido or Kelly. He knew they were connected to the Cartel and somehow found him. When he and Merido were cell mates, Merido would always share war stories that he had been through and it reminded JC of some shit on TV. It was intense and brutal, and he was a guy whose wrong side nobody would want to be on for sure. He never thought he would have been up against him because they were so close the whole time he was locked up, but soon as he was released, Merido had completely turned on him.

Chapter 11

After crawling on their stomachs for a good minute, he and Juicy finally made it to the back door. JC was breathing hard with exertion and was sweating buckets. He peeked out the window to see if anybody was in the back by the door they were about to open. He didn't see anyone. "Stay here, hold on," he told Juicy.

"No, don't leave me!" she whined, her voice high enough to carry outside.

"Quiet!" he told her urgently. "I don't want them to hear where we at, stay here baby, I'm just about to look."

Juicy had so many butterflies in her stomach, she didn't know what to do. Scared was an understatement. She had never been in the middle of anything like this in her entire life and she was scared half out of her mind. These people sounded to her like they had army guns and it didn't seem like they were planning on stopping anytime soon. She winced as a bullet flew right above her head and buried itself in the wall pushing plaster and dust out into the air. That was such a close one that she felt like she could hardly breathe.

Even though bullets were flying right over his head, JC was able to take a look outside. He saw seven guys dressed head to toe in all black holding machine guns and spraying the house with bullets. They were dressed up and had bullet proof vests under their clothes, with black ski masks pulled over their heads like they had been hired to do the job and didn't want to get identified. The van they drove was all black too, with no windows. Even the rims on it were black.

Once he had taken it all in, JC crawled back over to Juicy. "I think they just in the front. Look, I'ma open this door, ok? And on three, I want you to run as fast as you can, into the neighbors back yard..." Shots started ringing out again right by them but still none of them had managed to land a shot on either of them.

With that, he quickly opened the door. He saw the fear etched all over Juicy's face. She looked like she had already been shot. "Baby, on the count of three you hear me? 1...2...3 let's go." They both busted out the door together as the shots continued to ring out. Once they were out in the open, they ran as fast as they could. Juicy ran on ahead like he'd told her to do and JC was behind her, right on her heels. He felt two bullets zoom right pass his ear, almost clipping the shell. It was so close that he could feel the wind and heat of the bullet but by some miracle, it didn't hit him. The sound gave him the shivers. They kept running until they were in front of the neighbor's house. Both of them were breathing hard and their mouths had dried up so bad that their voices sounded different, they were so cracked and hoarse.

Chapter 12

"JC, what is going on?" Juicy cried between exhausted pants.

He looked around cautiously to see if they had been followed." Do you know anyone on this street? We gotta get off the street."

"No! I don't fucking know these people! I don't know anyone around here!" she shouted back at him and swung on him.

"What the fuck is wrong with you? Calm the fuck down and listen to me!" he shouted, gripping her shoulders and squeezing them, hoping to calm her down.

"No! Tell me what the fuck is going on! Why is these people trying to kill us!"

"They not trying to kill you, they trying to kill me! Now come on!" He reached for her arm, and she yanked away before he could grab hold of it.

"Well we need to split," she said as tears continued to fall from her eyes. Her face was puffy and her eyes was fire red. They both were drenched with sweat.

"Juicy, they came to your mom's house, looking for me. So obviously they know who you is. So it's best that we don't split so we can get the fuck out of here, come on."

"No! Why is these people trying to kill you! What did you do!"

"Bitch we can talk about that later, come the fuck on!" he shouted, running up on her again and pulling her along with him. "What the fuck is wrong with you? You think I'm about to stand in the middle of the street and explain this shit?" He was pissed off by how she was reacting. She was being stubborn and putting them both in danger.

"Bitch? Really? Let me go!" She was fighting him and trying to pull away.

"You a stupid bitch!"

"Fuck you, JC! Get away from me!"

"Bitch, you got my baby, come the fuck on, you dumb ass bitch!" He reached out and grabbed her by her hair. "Run!" When he yanked her hair, she stopped struggling and looked at his face. His eyes were stone cold red and he looked like the devil to her. That was when she knew he wasn't playing with her. He had her hair wrapped very tight in his hands and he tugged on it to make her start running.

"Let my fucking hair go!" she shouted, letting her legs collapse underneath her to make herself fall forward on purpose, causing him to let go.

"You a dumb ass bitch, I should kick you in your shit!" The gun shots had stopped and he was sure that the armed men could be pulling up at any moment. "Fuck you, you aint about to get me killed," he shouted as he turned away and started to walk away from her.

"You bitch ass nigga, you just gone leave me here!" she screamed after him, crying as he walked further and further away from her. She had scraped her knee and it was bleeding a little. She looked around and saw people looking out their windows, watching the whole argument. Tired and devastated, she just sat there on the side of the road and JC never turned back around to come get her or even check to see if she was okay. As soon as she saw him jogging away and disappearing between some houses, she stood up and got back on the sidewalk, then started walking the opposite way, holding her leg which was still aching and bleeding. She had left her cell phone and everything else back in the house. She was praying to God as she walked up the street. She thanked him that she didn't get hit.

Chapter 13

Seconds later, she saw a black van driving around the corner slowly. Once it caught up to her, two guys jumped out with huge guns pointed at her, blocking her path. "Please don't shoot me!" she begged as she put her hands up in front of her in a defensive gesture.

"Bitch, get in!" They grabbed her right up and threw her in the van before she could even register what was happening. When she realized she was being taken, she kicked and screamed, but she was not strong enough to overpower the huge men. They started tying her up, hands, then her legs, then they tied a rag around her mouth to keep her from screaming and attracting any unwanted attention.

JC jumped a few fences and was walking across a few back yards when he heard gun shots again. Thinking that he had been followed and tracked down, he took off running and ducking, sprinting at top speed through all the houses until he realized where the shots were coming from. His blood ran cold and his heart started beating violently in his chest, almost jumping right out like in a cartoon. The van was going the same way he was and a guy was shooting out of the window as he saw JC running across the lawns. Wanting to get them off his scent, JC stopped and ran the opposite way. Seconds later, the van was reversing down the street, the men inside still spraying bullets in his direction.

The few kids that were outside had gone inside their houses, scared for their lives. Even the dogs in the neighborhood had started barking, wondering what was going on. So many bullets were flying and JC was trying to get out the way somehow and dodge them while he ran. He had never ran this fast in his whole life. His heart was beating so fast that he felt lightheaded as adrenaline pumped through his body. As he ran, he wondered if they had got Juicy.

Finally, when he was completely out of breath and needed a rest before he passed out, he stopped again and hid behind a house which they were shooting up. He ran straight, hopping over another fence, to another street. There was a Pitbull right behind him as soon as he landed. He outran the dog, and hopped over the next fence to make his way to the front of the next house. There were people sitting on the porch, and they turned and looked at him like he was crazy. They saw JC sweating and out of breath, looking like he was a hunted rabbit. They had heard the gun shots, but didn't know they were as close as they were.

Every time JC heard the gun shots stop, he knew they were driving because they kept getting closer so quickly it was hard for him to keep up. After trying to catch his breath, he took off running across the street to another back yard and hid in some bushes. He crouched down and covered himself with the thick branches as best he could, making sure not to move around too much and rustle the leaves which could potentially give his hiding spot away. "Fuck," he mumbled. The bush was thick and he was getting poked by sticks from every direction. Carefully reaching down, he dug his phone out of his pocket and texted Linda to send him Sandra's number. He turned his phone up and watched the screen carefully, waiting for it to light up with a message. When he got a message with Sandra's number, he quickly called her.

Chapter 14

"Hello," Sandra's voice came down the line.
"Hey, what you doing? This JC." He was speaking
as low as he could.

"Who?"

He couldn't believe it. "JC, the guy that left your house this
morning," he said, trying not to sound impatient. He needed
her help after all.

"Ohh!" she laughed. "I didn't know who you were, I
never seen this number before."

"Where you at? You think you can come pick me
up?"

"Umm, from where?"

"I don't know. Can I let you know, in about ten
minutes? I don't know this area, so I couldn't give you
directions if I wanted to." He waited for her to say
something, hoping she'd say yes.

"It's ok, go to your text as if you was sending me a
text message. I'm going to show you how to send me your
location, then I can come right to you."

JC breathed a sigh of relief. He slowly parted the leaves of the bush and looked around to see if anyone was coming by him. His hands were shaking hard as he opened his messages and followed her instructions. He was able to do it successfully within seconds. "Ok if I move, will you still be able to get to me?"

"Yes, I will follow it until I see you. Are you ok? You sound like you out of breath." She sounded a little concerned, and JC quickly tried to sound less breathy.

"Yea, I'm fine. I was getting chased by a dog." He laughed. "A damn Pitbull nearly bit my pants off."

She busted out in laughter, but JC wasn't trying to stay on the phone. "Be on your way," he said before he hung up. He looked around again. The coast seemed to be clear and he couldn't hear the van or gun shots anymore. Then, he hopped out and started running again. He made it onto another street and came to a screeching halt when he saw the van was sitting right on the side of the road. Turning on his heel in an instant, he doubled back the opposite way but it was too late. The men had seen him and started to follow him again, and the chase continued. Bullets rang out again as JC was jumping fences and running as fast as he could. He began sprinting to save his wind. He had to get away from them on foot even if it seemed damn near impossible at the moment. He knew he had to somehow get out of this area before they cornered him. He thought about running into someone's house but instead he went inside an open garage and hid behind a car. He turned his phone on vibrate and just waited until Sandra called.

Chapter 15

He thought about the dream he had when he pulled up to Juicy's mom's house. It was like the dream was trying to tell him something, or warn him about what was going to happen. He found it weird and tried not to think about it too much because if he got distracted now, he just might get captured. The garage stank of stale fumes and old boxes, but it felt safe compared to out in the open. He kept texting Sandra to see how far she was but he had a while to wait. At least 45 minutes by the looks of it. He knew he had to get the hell out of Atlanta before he got himself killed or locked up. While he sat there, he thought about Juicy and even though she had pissed him off, he was hoping she was still alive especially being that she had his baby inside of her.

After 30 minutes of waiting, his phone started to vibrate. Thinking that Sandra had somehow made it there sooner, he looked at the screen, ready to pick up the call. Then he saw that it wasn't Sandra. He was getting a call from Juicy, but he didn't answer. He didn't know if the guys were outside of the garage or what. He didn't want to make a sound so he texted her instead.

JC: Hold on a minute.

Juicy: Answer the fucking phone!

JC: Ok, give me a second. Are you ok?

Juicy: This not Juicy.

JC: I know.

They started calling again but JC just ended it again. There was no way he was talking to the guy on the other end of the line. They'd got Juicy already and now they were out to get him. He sat there hoping no one would come inside the garage. He needed a weapon so he started looking around. The musty old garage was filled with old things shoved inside boxes and a few gardening tools in the back. He saw a couple of rakes and a couple shovels. It was better than having nothing so he grabbed a shovel and sat back down behind the car, shovel grasped firmly in one hand. After all the shit he had been through, he didn't want it to end like this. He imagined himself at least going out in a shootout or even a fist fight. But not just being without a gun when everyone else has guns, and being shot down dead like a dog on the street, defenseless. He was slipping and he was mad at himself.

A call came through, and it was Sandra. "Hello," he whispered. "Where are you?"

"I think I'm here. I'm not sure. Where are you? And why are you whispering? I'm here for sure."

Chapter 16

JC got up from his hiding place and started walking to the front of the garage and looking out a small window. He still whispered into the phone, "Do you see a black van where you are?"

"A black van?" She looked around, and up and down the street. "No, no black van. Where are you? I'm like in the hood right now, people looking out their windows. It's pretty creepy."

JC slowly walked out, looking both ways, while holding the shovel. He noticed Sandra as soon as he stepped in front of the drive way because of her ride. "Are you driving this fancy ass sports car?"

"It's a Ferrari. Yes. Where are you?" After she got her last word out, he was at the door. He was all dirty, and had leaves all over his clothes. He jumped in and slammed the door shut.

"Go," he said as he tried to lean his seat back. She took right off, and jumped on the freeway.

"Let me show you what this baby can do," she grinned, as she sped off onto the freeway like a bat out of hell.

****

Later that day, Juicy was brought to a huge house in Atlanta. She was still crying, her face puffed up and streaked with tears, when they brought her in. "So how you meet this nigga Juicy? I thought you was smarter than that. This nigga going to get you killed," Nino said as he sat at the marble dinner table across from her. They had untied her feet and her mouth so she could walk on her own and answer Nino's questions. One of the guys had to choke her out before they brought her there because she wouldn't stop screaming her lungs raw.

Chapter 17

"I met him through Gloria. I don't even know this nigga. Why are you trying to kill this nigga like this?" Juicy asked, her voice shuddering. "You shot up my car? My momma's house? What the fuck?"

"That's what happens when you around the wrong company," Nino shrugged as he eyed her. "You coulda got hit or your mom coulda even got hit. I'm glad that you didn't though, because as you already know, I been had a crush on you for a long time now, but I guess I'm not your type. But that's cool. Anyway, where can I find JC?"

Juicy was pissed. She frowned and pursed her lips. She wanted to spit in his face but she knew better than to do that right now.

"I don't know where he would go. I don't know anything about him honestly. I'm scared and I don't know what he did or what's going on, I swear." She began to cry again, her face crumpling as she sobbed.

"He killed a couple of my people. More than a couple actually. This nigga is not the nigga you should have been around, Juicy," Nino told her sternly.

"Gloria was messing with him, and I know how she is, so I assumed he was good," Juicy sniffled.

"You see where Gloria is, right?"

More tears fell from her eyes onto the fancy carpet on the dining room floor, and she started praying that nothing bad would happen to her. "Just please, Nino, believe me. You know I am not about no street shit outside of the strip club. I just get my money and stay out the way. Don't put me in JC shit." She looked around at the three other guys standing around.

Nino dialed JC's number again and he finally answered.

"What's up?" JC answered.

"So I got your bitch. What you want me to do with her?" Nino asked bluntly.

"Keep it street, wait until you run into me. She aint got nothing to do with shit. Let her go. This between me and you. You know what it is when we cross paths again."

"So that's your word? This between me and you right?"

"Fasho."

Nino hung up and told one of his guys to drop Juicy off to wherever she was going. He told her that he would get her mom's crib back together as well. He knew deep down if he would have did something to Juicy, JC would have went for his mom and other family members. He had enough problems going on already and didn't want to add to them.

Chapter 18

JC laid in the bed in deep thought. He was mad at Juicy because they could have used her as a bargain chip because she was stubborn and let herself get caught. That's how he had lost Brittany. He started having flash backs about when it happened. Atlanta was too dangerous of a place for him to be now that he was beefing with Nino. He had no idea about all the people Nino knew, and he didn't want to get caught slipping. He wanted to leave. He had to leave.

"Are you ok? You want some head?" Sandra asked, nudging him gently.

JC shook his head. "Just leave me be. I'ma chill and figure out what I really want to do. I may have to get out of Atlanta."

"What actually happened? It can't be that bad."

"I was messing with a known person wife. Now he's after me. I came here to have peace, not be in a war, so I need to go."

Sandra nodded understandingly. "Where would you go?"

"I don't know. Anywhere. I'm not sure just yet though."

"I'm going with you then," she said, smiling.

JC laughed and shook his head disbelievingly. "Yeah right. You got this good ass life out here. Ain't no reason for you to leave."

"What if I like you and want to help you with things. I know you going to need money. I have that. I know you going to need a white girl with good credit to get you a place and other things. I can do all that. I mean, you have good dick, you cute, you have a big dick and you like having sex like me. I think we perfect." She looked at him with her eyes soft. She wasn't kidding and that took him by surprise.

JC laughed again. "You tripping, your mom will kill you if you steal her dick away," he joked.

"Fuck that bitch. I owe her one anyway. She probably fucked some of my other boyfriends that I never found out about," she grumbled, wrinkling her nose at the thought.

"You crazy. So you trying to rock with me?"

"Rock with you? What's a rock?"

"It means, you tryna fuck with me, be with me, basically," he explained. This girl wasn't street. She had had everything all her life, born with a silver spoon.

"Oh yeah," she giggled. "You going to have to help me out with the slang thing. I don't know much slang."

"No worries, you good." He started thinking about what she was saying. He could go somewhere and get himself together easily, using her. She had the money and influence to get him a fresh new start. Then he thought again, he wanted to get to Merido and Kelly. He didn't feel like just running away to hide out. He wanted to kill. He wanted revenge. Sandra would only get in his way and become another witness to what he was actually trying to take care of. He had a couple more days until Linda came back, to think about what he was going to do and what move he wanted to make. He wanted to get out of Atlanta. He knew he wasn't going to be able to get to Nino right now. Nino was on high alert and things needed to die down first. He needed to get some money, which he was sure he could just get from Sandra or even Linda when she came back.

"So that's your car you picked me up in?"

"Yes. I love sports cars. That's a Ferrari F12 Berlinetta. It's my baby. I have a Lamborghini too. I love cars," she said as she giggled.

"Your ass, spoiled as hell I see. I wish I had some rich parents. My parents didn't even buy me a car at all. I come from the hood, that's something you probably don't know much about."

"I'm not going to lie. I love having sex with hood guys. It's so different. It's way more aggressive. It feels like someone angry is fucking me. I think it's so awesome," she confessed, licking her lips as she eyed him up and down again.

JC laughed at how thirsty she was. Sandra was always saying some crazy shit. He liked her personality, but he knew they could only talk about certain things since she wouldn't be able to relate much.

"So why didn't your parents buy you a car? Not even after you graduated?"

"Well I'm a foster kid."

Her heart dropped.

"Oh wow. What happened?"

"My mom didn't want me when I was born, I guess. I went to a foster home. I was such a bad kid though. My foster parents was cool, but I was a devil."

"That's really sad. I'm so sorry to hear that."

"It's all good. I'm hungry as hell. Can we get some food?" she asked. JC could hear a small rumble coming from his stomach.

"Yea, what you want?"

"Steak and potatoes."

"I know just the spot. You want me to go grab it, or you cool with delivery?"

"Delivery is cool. You smoke?"

"Hell yea."

"You look like one of them stoner ass white girls. I knew you smoked. Ya'll got some good shit out here in Atlanta?"

"No. But I get good shit sent to me from Cali. One second." she went to her room and grabbed some different flavors of weed and showed JC. She had a real good selection and all the paraphernalia that came with it. It was an organized collection too in a pretty little girly box. It made JC smile.

Chapter 19

"Oh yeah, you got the good shit. You a real stoner. You got your little grinder and everything in this box."

They both laughed.

"I'll roll some up. You smoke blunts, right?"

JC laughed. "That's all I smoke. I'm a nigga. That's what we do. I'm surprise you smoke blunts, you look like you smoke bongs and shit."

She giggled, biting her lip gently and brushing a strand of hair away from her face. "The funny thing is, I never even smoked out of one of those. I have black friends, I'm not all that white. If I was like this little scared white girl-."

"Hold on, hold on, I never said you was a scared white girl. I've known that from the first day I met your ass. You pulled my dick out and was like let's fuck."

She cracked up at that, laughing up a storm. "Oh my God. I was so stoned that night. I was doing coke that night. When I'm on coke I just get so fucking horny I just want to like hump everything I see. If you wouldn't have fucked me, I would have literally tried to force you to. I had been in my room playing with my dildo for so long, I needed some dick so bad, I didn't know what to do."

"Damn it makes you feel like that?"

"Yes, especially after hearing how loud you was fucking my mom," she confessed.

"Why didn't you call some dick over?"

"My boyfriend's in the army. When you came in, we was on a video call. He was jacking off, while I was fucking myself."

"Oh wow, so what you tell him when you just left out the room like that?"

"What you mean, what did I tell him?"

"You left out the room, talking to me and went downstairs and fucked me. Was he still on video when you came back?"

"Of course he was. He didn't say anything. I continued to play with myself when I came back."

"That nigga dumb as fuck, I woulda been like, bitch who is that?" he laughed, astonished.

"Nooo! He's not like that at all," she told him. "He trust me. He send me all the money he makes in the Army, plus he loves me."

They both laughed.

"He's white?"

"Yes."

"How many black dudes you been with?" JC was interested to know how he compared with the other guys who fucked her.

"You're the 6th one."

"He don't even care that your dildo big and black like that?" He shook his head, amazed.

Chapter 20

She laughed and shook her head. "No, he don't care. He has the same size dick as you, and he's a white boy. Black was the only color they had when I got that one."

JC laughed disbelievingly, "Oh damn, he packing like that?"

"Yea man. I love his dick. He's has a bigger dick then the other 5 black guys I fucked. You and him like a tie."

"Every black guy don't have the biggest dick. That ain't always true."

"Yea I see, but I don't care about the size always. Now I will tell you one thing. You fuck way better than my boyfriend. He has a big dick, but I have to always make myself cum. You actually can make me cum the way you be fucking me. So size is not always a thing for me. I like to be fucked good."

"I see. I didn't think your little ass was going to be able to take my dick as good as you be taking it. You proved me wrong."

She smiled. She was clearly up for the challenge. "Yes, I can take it." She sounded confident and JC found it endearing.

"I was going easy on you though," he warned her teasingly.

"Oh really, why is that?" she asked flirtatiously, batting her lashes.

"Just because, you so little."

"Skinny?"

"Yea."

"Naw I can take it. I probably can take you in my ass. Long as you not going crazy. You have to be gentle. Me and my boyfriend do that all the time. That's the only way he can make me cum honestly."

"Oh damn, that's crazy. I heard that from a few girls. That in their ass hole is the only way they can have an orgasm." He had heard about it but he'd never actually seen it, which made him more curious about her.

"I have a friend name Kelly that can only orgasm by being fucked in her ass."

JC's stomach dropped when he heard that name. "Kelly white?" he asked, trying to keep his voice from sounding too concerned.

"Yea, she's the best. I love her so much," Sandra said.

"She from Atlanta? Well lives in Atlanta?"

"Yes born and raised." She paused at the look on JC's face. "You know her? She for sure knows a lot of people. I wouldn't be surprised."

He thought about it for a second. "You have a picture of her?" Kelly had lied to him so much. He needed to see what this Kelly looked like to be sure.

49

Chapter 21

"Yes, she's beautiful." Sandra scrolled through her phone and showed him a picture.

"Oh naw, I never seen her before, but she's a cutie." The tension that had filled his body at the mention of Kelly's name eased and he let out a deep sigh. He was relieved to see it wasn't the one he was thinking about. "I'll put this dick in her ass for sure."

"She will so let you too. She loves her some black guys."

"I had some bad luck with Kellys, I wouldn't even want to deal with another one. Bad experience."

Sandra giggled, as she licked the blunt. "So what do you love? Like, what are you into?"

"One thing I love is guns."

"Guns? My dad was into guns. We have so many of his guns."

"For real? You have some of his guns here?"

"Yea. You wanna see some? I don't know anything about any of them but I'll show you some."

He followed Sandra to her mother's closet which was huge. She opened the closet to reveal a huge collection of guns, probably the most expensive ones he'd ever seen. There were some in glass cases and he assumed there were more inside the lockboxes. These weren't the type that anyone he knew used. They were brand new and carefully maintained, and just one look told him that they probably cost a fortune. "There are some in here. My mom keeps them in here for her safety although I don't believe she will ever shoot anyone. I'm a pussy but I think I will shoot a gun before she tries to."

They both laughed at that. JC saw a few fancy boxes that looked fireproof. He opened them one by one and saw some of the best 45 caliber guns he had ever seen. These guns were special, and he could tell they cost money. He started picking them up, they had nice bullets and all. Extra clips as well. "I love these two," he said, sliding his fingers over the guns.

"Oh my God. Don't think I'm weird, but you look so sexy with those guns. I just wanna suck the shit out your dick right now, dude," Sandra gasped as she eyed him holding the guns, her pupils dilated with arousal.

He laughed, shaking his head. "You silly as hell. I need to get some of these."

"You can have those. Pick whatever you want," she said with a slight shrug. "My mom won't fucking ever notice. My dad has like hundreds of guns. Come, I'll show you more. Where's a fucking lighter?" she looked around for a lighter to light the blunt. She lit it and puffed it a few times before leaving the room. JC followed her to another room where more guns were stored. It was a huge room that had deer heads mounted on the walls all around it, as well as rifles and more hunting stuff too. This was a room dedicated to her dad and it had all his favorite stuff inside. There was a

51

pool table as well in the middle of the floor. Sandra walked over to a closet and opened it and there were guns inside everywhere. This guy had practically every gun you could think of from small to big. They all were hanging up on each side of the walls. The rifles were set on the floor. Then there were plenty of fancy boxes stacked up, which had one of a kind guns inside. JC spent about 45 minutes inside there looking through all the boxes and admiring the guns while they smoked and talked about who her dad was. JC even found himself two better guns and she told him he could have them. That pleased him a lot since those guns would definitely come in handy.

Chapter 22

"You sure your mom not going to find out and beat your ass?" he asked her.

She giggled, "She's not going to find out unless you tell her. And she's not going to beat my ass. They're yours."

"Thanks," JC got him some extra bullets and clips too. He wished he would have had some of this stuff earlier, he woulda been able to at least shoot back, but most of all, feel safer. He wanted to fight back and he had the equipment for it now if he was in a situation like that again, though he hoped he wouldn't be. They walked back to Linda's room.

"Lets go in my room instead of here. I see you keep going right back to my moms room like you scared. Make yourself at home."

JC laughed and followed her to her room. She walked straight over to her small table where she snorted some coke up her nose. "You party?" she asked as she held the tray out for him to take some too.

"No, not me."

"Have you ever tried it?"

"No."

"Why not? Come on, live a little. This is the good shit." She wiped the white residue off her nose and grinned at him.

JC laughed and held a hand up. "Naw, I'm good. I never wanted to try it. I don't do anything besides smoke weed and drink."

"Party pooper," Sandra hummed, sniffing the remnants of the powder covering the insides of her nostrils. "More for me then. Don't say I didn't ask."

The door bell rang shrill and loud through the house, and Sandra went downstairs. She grabbed the food she had ordered and brought it all upstairs. They sat down and ate and talked more. "Can you have someone bring me some underwear and shit? I don't have anything. I need hygiene products and all," JC said. He had sweated so much after running away from the guys with the guns. He was desperate for a shower.

"Hell yea, I'll have my bitch Greg do it," Sandra told him with a grin.

"Your bitch Greg?"

"He's gay, don't worry. He's cool. Gossip queen but he's cool. Just write everything that you need down and I'll text him. Matter fact, text him the list from my phone. Tell him everything you want and the size, and give me back the phone before you send it."

"Ok bet."

"Put whatever you want. He does anything I tell him to do," she told him, flipping her hair over her shoulder.

"Damn you got it like that?"

"Heck yea, watch. When we send him this message, I'll call him and talk to him. I'll tell him to get his ass up from whatever he's doing and hurry up."

She sent the message and waited about 2 minutes before she was calling him.

"Helllooo." A high tinny voice came down the line.

"Why didn't you respond bitch?"

"Bitch, I'm in the middle of trying to get some dick. What do you want anyway?" he asked in a very feminine voice.

"I need you to do something. This is urgent. Like yesterday bitch, you can suck dick later. I need this done. Chop, chop, you know I'm going to take care of you."

"You going to take care of me good or good good?"

"I'm going to take care of you good, good, good! Now get over here."

"I'm on it, bitch, bye!"

Chapter 23

The guy hung up and Sandra tossed her phone away with a satisfied smile that said mission accomplished.

"What the hell does good, good, good mean?" JC asked, confused by the conversation between them.

She laughed and shook her head. "It means, I'm going to give him good money, coke, weed and whatever else he wants. Sometimes he asks to borrow one of my cars. We shall see."

"Damn, that's what's up. See this how I want to live. Just make a muthafucka fuck up their whole plans for what you need or want them to do." JC laughed.

"Oh yeah for sure. One time, he was at the airport picking up his boyfriend, and I told him that I needed something and I'll pay him $500. He left his boyfriend at the airport and told him to take a Uber," Sandra said with a giggle. "His boyfriend hates me because he thinks I'm a selfish, spoiled brat. I don't give a fuck."

JC laughed. This girl was unbelievable. "Damn, you out cold for that."

"Fuck him. He cheats on Greg and gets caught all the fucking time," she shot back.

JC just shook his head while rolling up another blunt. "This a big ass tv you got. What size is that?"

"85 inch, it's huge man. I love this tv," she said, sitting back and staring at the giant screen.

"So, you just be chilling all day in the house? What you be doing for fun normally? Like if I wasn't here. What would you be doing?" JC was curious about what kind of life Sandra led. She had all the money she needed, surely she wouldn't spend all her time hanging around her house.

"I'd be fucking playing with my pussy if you wasn't here," she told him with a little bit of attitude, biting back a grin.

JC laughed at that. "What would you do after that?"

"Maybe go to the mall shopping. I don't know. I don't really do much. I really spend a lot of time at home. Sometimes friends come over. Or I'll be on facetime with my boyfriend, that's about it." She got up and walked over to a small bar in the corner. "Do you like whiskey? I have some bomb whisky? I'm talking like the best shit."

"Yea I'll try it."

She went and got some glasses and poured for them both. They started drinking and smoking again. She played some music in the background, and they chilled all the way until Greg came and dropped all JC's stuff off. He had even brought him back two outfits and some shoes. "Damn he hooked it up," JC said, impressed by all the things he had just gotten.

"Well, I took a peek at your shoe size and told him to bring you some clothes too." Greg had got him some nice Nike sweat suits to wear, nothing fancy, but comfortable.

57

After he left, they both took showers, and went downstairs to where they had an indoor swimming pool, and a hot tub. It all looked super luxurious and just looking at the room made JC feel more relaxed. It was hard to forget the dreams he had and the shootout, but this sure helped get his mind off a few things.

Chapter 24

"Damn, this is nice as hell." JC's eyes lit up as he admired the room. "So you rich, rich I see. This ain't no regular shit."

"Thank you." she said, stepping into the hot tub brimming with bubbles. There were 6 tv's all around the room and this was the safest JC had felt in a while. There was no way anyone would find him here.

"This living right here," he said, smiling broadly as he got ready to enter the hot tub. He took off his shirt, and stepped into the hot tub holding his drink above water. "This shit dope."

"I know right. I just be feeling so free sometimes when I be in here. It's just so peaceful and relaxing. You ever fucked in a hot tub before?" She had that look in her eye like she was getting some ideas.

"Yes, have you?" JC quirked an eyebrow at her.

"Of course. You ever fucked a white girl in a hot tub before?" she countered immediately, as she took off her top, revealing her perfect tits. JC's eyes fixed on the pink nipples that were shining with the water from the hot tub.

"Naw, naw, she wasn't white," he said with a small shurg, not taking his eyes off what was in front of him. They were both buzzing hard and had been smoking weed for some hours now. She walked over to him slowly to let him savor the moment, and started kissing him and his dick woke up. She backed up and started taking her bottoms off. Her bikini bottoms were already skimpy as hell and once she untied the strings on either side, the material fell right off.

"I don't think I'll need these in here," she said, tossing them on the side.

"Yea, you may not need those. I may not need these neither." With that, he took off his shorts as well and tossed them to the side. She came closer to him, kissing him and climbing up on him as he slid his dick smoothly inside her. She motioned up and down while holding onto his shoulders for support as she bounced on his dick.

"Oh my God, you feel so fucking good," she moaned, riding his dick as he palmed her ass. "Yes, baby, right there. Right there feel so fucking good," she moaned loudly still moving up and down non stop.

He walked around with her while still fucking her nice and slow. She seemed to be enjoying it more than he was. The water took away some of the sensation for him but he kept going.

"Yes baby, you're fucking me so good. Don't stop," she moaned. She kept riding and riding, then started licking all over his bald head and moaning, "Yesss, baby, yesss, this dick is good, baby. Fuck me harder, baby," she whined, and he complied as he put more force in his stroke, slamming her down on his dick, gutting her insides, filling up every inch of her.

"Yes!" she shouted still bouncing up and down holding onto him tighter and turning red in the face. "Yes! Yes! Yes! Fuck me! Fuck me! Fuck me!"

Chapter 25

JC's veins were starting to pop out of his strong arms as he guided her up and down on his dick, holding her firmly by her hips. She wasn't heavy at all, so he was able to do this non stop and it was driving her crazy. Her voice was echoing throughout the whole room as she held on for dear life. "Fuck yea! Fuck yea! I'm cumming! I'm cumming!" she screamed until she felt her body shaking uncontrollably, almost shaking right out of his arms. "Shittttt! Baby! Shittttt!" she screamed as he kept pumping into her while she lost total control of her body.

He was bouncing her up and down like a rag doll, "Take it," he said aggressively, still pumping his thick shaft inside of her. He started going faster and faster trying to make himself cum, but it still wasn't cumming even after all that.

"Shit! Baby shit! You killing me! Shit!" she screamed as she still felt his dick slamming inside her wet pussy. She held on but her eyes were rolling in the back of her head. He just kept pumping and pumping to the point she was about to reach another orgasm soon. "Baby! Baby! Baby!" she screamed, digging her fingers in the skin of his back, leaving small grooves. She no longer had any strength in her legs. They were just hanging over his arms as he was still pumping into her, his hips bucking and driving his dick deep into her. He was growling like a hungry lion as he was fighting to reach his nut. It took a few more minutes before he finally came, and he lifted her up high enough right up to where his dick fell out into the water as he nutted. The cum raced into the water, clouding it up a little.

They both were breathing hard, and Sandra was shaking like she couldn't stop. "Do not put me down," she said, wrapping her arms around his neck to hold on tight. "I'm positive I can't fucking walk right now. Oh my God."

JC let out a laugh, as he was breathing hard with exertion after thrusting into her. He set her on top of the edge of the hot tub and she reached for her drink, taking a long gulp as she crossed her legs. "I'm about to take a dive in the pool." He got up a bit unsteadily and dove in, swimming to the other side then swimming back. Sandra was still sitting where he left her at and was drinking her drink. She was still in a daze and she looked completely exhausted.

"I see what you meant, when you said you was taking it easy on me. I might have underestimated what you could do with that thing," she said.

JC smiled, lifting himself out the pool butt naked, obliging her. His dick was still somewhat hard and swinging. "What you talking about?"

"You just almost killed me!" she said, rolling her eyes. "OMG, you are dangerous. I never thought I would say this in my life, but don't ever fuck me like that unless you want to be stuck forever. Fuck me how you fucked me the first couple times. That's good enough."

JC laughed. "You said you wanted me to turn up."

"That's too much. Too fucking much, dude." She waved her hand in the air. She was tipsy and slurring her words a little bit. The glass in her hand looked like it would tip out at any second.

"You good? What you over there thinking about?"

"Breaking up with my boyfriend," she blurted out.

JC busted out in laughter. "Man, shut up!" he said playfully. "You so dramatic."

"I'm so fucking serious. He needs to step his sex game up," she whined. "He has too much dick to not be fucking me better. The way you just fucked me is how I need to be fucked. That's why I'm constantly wanting to have sex. Right now, I'm fine. I don't want any more dick. I'm good. My pussy is wrecked."

"That pussy wrecked?" JC tilted his head and looked at the spot between the vee of her thighs.

"Yes," she said as she looked at him with puppy eyes.

"Who wrecked that pussy sweetheart?" he asked, coaxing her to respond to his question.

"You," she said, pointing at him as he was stepping back in the hot tub. He came up to her, and uncrossed her legs for her. He spread them, and kissed her pussy twice.

"Who?"

"You did."

"I did?" he said, kissing her pussy again and again, letting his tongue drag over the sensitive pink flesh moist with pool water and her juices. He kissed around her clit, letting his tongue slip out through his lips just a little bit.

"Yes, you did," she said, as her breathing got heavier and she was panting in gentle bursts of air. "That feels so good."

JC licked her clit softly, making small circles around it with the tip of his tongue. Her pussy lips were still open like he had stretched her out and it needed more time to close. He made bigger circles around her clit next and it drove her crazy. "Yesss, baby!" she moaned, grabbing the back of his head, her fingers slightly digging into his bald head. She had one leg thrown up and he was eating her pussy so good, she never wanted him to stop.

"That pussy starting to feel a little better?" he asked her, as he sucked on her clit while licking slowly.

"Yesss, so good," she moaned with a smile, biting down on her lip, holding his head right in the spot that felt like heaven to her.

JC pulled back, and started licking her thighs and kissing the soft, smooth skin there. He bit them gently while looking her in the eyes. She was looking down at him with a confused look on her face that was bright red. He saw her on edge like she wanted him to put his face back in, but he made her beg for it.

"Please suck my clit again," she asked longingly, as her heart rate picked up, her blood pumping down to heat up the tender spot between her legs.

JC went back to sucking her clit, and soon she was shaking, gripping his head, screaming as she came so hard. "Shit!!!"

Chapter 26

As JC backed away, wiping his mouth, he dipped his head in the hot tub and came back up. "You good now?"

"Good? I'm fantastic." She finished the rest of her glass of whiskey in a few big sips, and it seemed to make her even mellower. They sat and talked until about 4am. JC shared a little about his life with her and where he came from and she did the same with him. They had a good vibe going the whole night and finally made their way upstairs to her bedroom where they went straight to sleep until the next morning.

When JC woke up, he saw the screen of his phone lighting up with several notifications. Gazing at it with sleep blurred eyes, he saw that he had several missed calls and text messages from Juicy.

Juicy: When I first met you, I thought you was this cool ass nigga. You had my back, you showed me respect, and you made me feel like you really liked me. As we got to know each other, you made me feel like you loved me. You was really a good nigga in my eyes. But I guess everything is not what they appear to be. You really left me in the middle of a death trap, me and your unborn baby. You ain't shit, and not going to be shit. Good thing I knew who Nino is otherwise, fucking with you, I would be dead right now. You can keep ignoring my phone calls and text all you want, but you know deep down inside, you are a hoes ass nigga. You left me! You left us! And you a wanted nigga, all over the news. You have articles and shit all over the internet. You are a demon. I can't believe I let you trick me into having any kind of feelings for you. I can honestly say I hate that I ever started loving you. I hate that I even met you. Don't bother responding, don't bother calling, don't bother doing nothing. Just keep running like you doing, because the shit you are wanted for, Karma going to hit your ass harder then I could ever hit you. Fuck you JC!

JC shook his head when he was done reading her message, she had sent other messages as well, but all they were saying is for him to pick up the phone. He wanted to respond and let her know he didn't leave her, but she was about to get them both killed. "Stupid bitch," he said and a low tone, trying to control his annoyance. He looked over at Sandra, and she was knocked out, lightly snoring. Her phone was vibrating as well. It was her mom. She kept calling, back to back. When she finally stopped, JC grabbed her phone and looked at Linda's text messages. She was asking if JC was still there and telling her that he was wanted for murder. And if she didn't call her back, she was going to send the police over to the house. He quickly dropped the phone.

"Sandra." JC rocked her awake urgently.

"Yes?" she asked drowsily, blinking and rubbing her eyes as she looked up at him questioningly.

"Your mom calling and texting you like crazy."

"She don't want shit. She's always calling like that and doesn't want shit," she said, turning over on her side and

67

closing her eyes back. She was getting comfortable to continue her nap but JC couldn't let that happen.

"Well this might be important. You may want to get this," he told her, holding out her phone which was ringing non stop.

"Oh my God." She turned around and grabbed her phone from JC, answering it in an irritated tone. "What, mom!"

Chapter 27

By the time Linda had revealed the news to her, JC had the gun pointed straight at her head. "Don't scream, relax, tell her I'm not here. I'm not going to kill you," he told her in a steady and calm voice.

For some reason she believed him because she nodded slightly. She was scared and confused but still said. "He's not here mom. Why would you send the police over?"

Finally, she hung up. "JC, what is going on?" she asked, fear and worry tinging her voice.

"I'm wanted for a murder."

"No, she said, multiple murders." Sandra sat up and looked at JC with a dubious look on her face.

"Ok multiple murders. For protecting my family, not just going around killing people," he told her as he still had his gun pointed at her.

"Listen, please put the gun down. I don't want anything to do with this. Just leave, and I'll forget I ever met you."

"No problem," he said as he was walking backwards. Before he got out the room, he heard banging at the door. It was loud and purposeful.

"Fuck, that's the police," she said with a scared look on her face.

JC's stomach clenched at the sound of the police right outside the door. "Call her and ask her if she told the police that I was here or not. Put her on speaker phone."

Sandra picked up the phone and dialed her mom back. "Hello."

"Mom, did you tell the police that he was here? They are at the door knocking right now."

"No of course not. I told them that you were in danger at the house before I talked to you. Just go tell them, there's no problem, and they will leave."

"Oh my God, mom. This so fucking stupid."

"I'm sorry, I thought he was still there and harming you or something. I don't know." She sounded apologetic, but that didn't seem to make Sandra any less annoyed.

"No, he's been gone. If he wanted to harm us, I'm sure he would have been done it."

There were heavy knocks at the door again. The rapping was more urgent now. JC was sure if Sandra didn't answer the door soon, they'd come busting in.

"Mom, can you at least call back and tell them to get the hell out of here before they kick the door in or something?"

"I'll try. Sorry about that. I was just trying to protect you. I'll call them right now."

Chapter 28

After about 5 minutes, the police were still beating on the door as if they knew someone was inside. Sandra and JC looked out a few windows and saw 12 cars out there, and two more were driving up. That was way more than JC could handle, even if he went out guns blazing. "How did they get inside the gate?" JC asked, still pointing his gun at her. It was always locked and it seemed suspicious to him that they had somehow just driven in.

"My mom must've gave them the code. Can you please put the gun down, you're fucking making me pretty nervous. I'm not going to turn you in. I don't think you're just a damn serial killer, otherwise, I'm sure you would have already killed me. We've been together for a while now."

JC didn't trust her of course. He lowered the gun from her face to her body. "I aint putting the gun down, but I'll take it off your head. We need to get these police up out of here."

"I'll just go down and answer the door and tell them, it was a false call," she told him.

"Slowly, lets go. Do not let them come inside. I'm telling you, it will get real messy. I'm not letting them just arrest me, so don't try anything funny. I promise you, you'll regret it." He made himself sound as threatening as he could so she wouldn't think about trying anything once they were downstairs.

Sandra swallowed hard and looked at him, balking at the hard expression on his face. "Ok. Ok." She started walking down the stairs. They still heard the knocks. It was like the police had no intentions of leaving. JC thought about how things would play out if they were to enter. He thought about his dream and how most of his dream was somewhat coming true. He wondered if this was the part where he get shot as many times as he got shot in his dreams. That scene replayed in his mind over and over again as he got closer and closer to the door. It seemed like some kind of premonition and the thought of it made him more nervous than he'd like to admit.

"Tell them, sorry, it was a false call," he whispered.

"What do you guys want out there and why are you at my door?" she yelled through the door.

"We got a call saying someone could be in danger here. So, we had to come out and check."

"Well call your supervisor and ask him if that was called off. Nobody's in danger here. I'm the only person here and I just got out of the shower, that you guys rudely interrupted!"

"Sorry ma'am, I'm just doing my job. So, you are the only person inside the house?" The cop sounded unconvinced.

"Yes."

"You mind if we take a quick look inside, it will only take about 40 seconds."

"No, you're not looking through my house. Leave, what the fuck is wrong with you guys? I'm going to call your fucking supervisor if you don't get off my property."

"Can you just come to the window or something and show me that you're ok."

"I just told you I just got out of the shower. You want to see me naked you pervert?"

"No, no, no not naked. Go put on some clothes please, and either just open the door and show us you ok, or come to the side window."

"I'm going to go to the window fucking naked, since he want to be a dick." She started taking off her clothes.

"What the hell you doing?" JC hissed, wondering what the hell she was doing.

"Fuck them." She got naked and went to the window and made contact with the officer. He covered his face right away when he saw that she really was naked. All the other guys watched as well and were surprised. "You happy now!" she shouted back angrily. "Now get off my fucking property!"

"Sorry, yes ma'am, sorry, have a good day." He backed off and told all the other guys to back off as well. They all put away their weapons, got back in their cars, drove off, and the gates closed behind them. It was only then that JC breathed a sigh of relief.

73

Chapter 29

"You are crazy," JC said, as he shook his head at her. Sandra picked up her clothes and walked up stairs with JC right behind her.

"Now what are you going to do? Do I need to take you somewhere? I will drop you wherever," she offered.

"Yea. Take me to a bus station where I don't need a I.D. to ride it."

"I know of one but it's really ghetto. The bus goes everywhere."

"That's cool, take me there please. You have any cash?"

"Here's $1000 bucks for you. Take it." She handed him the money from her wallet and then started getting dressed and gave him a backpack to put his clothes in as well. Her phone started ringing again. It was her mom again.

"Yes mom?"

"Did you walk in front of them butt ass naked?" Linda's voice was loud and shrill and JC could hear it too.

"Yea. They insisted that they see me so they could know I was safe. I told them I had just got out of the shower.

They acted like they was going to beat the fucking door down, so yes, I showed them my body."

"That's so embarrassing. You know I work along with the Sheriff. Why would you do that? How do I explain that, Sandra?"

"Just tell them I was drunk. No big deal. It's not like they never saw a naked woman before."

"That's not the point."

"I mean, it's your fault."

"Oh it's my fault? Really Sandra? Me looking out for your safety is my fault?"

"That was stupid mom," Sandra groaned at her mom. "Why would you call the police and send them here? Don't you think, if he was a serial killer, he woulda already did what he was going to do the first time he was here?"

"He may have changed his mind. I don't know. I don't know how killers think. As a mother, I just wanted to make sure you were safe."

Chapter 30

"Well thanks, a quarter of the Atlanta police department saw my new, perfect tits," she told her sarcastically.

"Not funny, Sandra. Oh, don't try to use your credit cards, I froze those too."

"Why!"

"I didn't know if he robbed you and took all your cards. I don't know. When Jamie called me with the news, I just wasn't thinking clear. I just reacted."

"Whelp. I'm safe. And I guess I'm broke until you get back."

"Stop it, Sandra. I can get you some money if you need anything. I'll make it up to you. I'm sorry."

"Make it up how?"

"I know you want the new Birkin bag that just came out. Maybe I'll get you that."

"If you get that, I won't be mad anymore."

"Done. Tell me you love me and not mad at me."

"Thanks. I love you and I'm not mad at you!"

"Bye, bitch!"

Sandra got off the phone happy and JC was just looking at her. "So that's how rich people do shit, huh? You spoiled as fuck," he said and they both laughed.

"That was bullshit and you know it. Why would you send the damn police to the house? She gave them the gate code and everything. She's always overly dramatic." Sandra sighed and pulled her shirt on over the tits she'd flashed to the police department.

"I mean, I feel you. You and your mom both crazy." JC shook his head with a chuckle.

They both laughed again. "You loved this little pussy though why it lasted, don't lie," she said teasingly to him, still feeling it after the pounding he'd given it.

"It was alright. Let's go." JC wasn't playing with her anymore. He was ready to get the hell out of there.

Finally, they made it to the same car she picked him up in. It was bound to catch people's attention and that's the last thing he needed now. "You don't have anything less flashy? I don't want to pull up in the ghetto in a damn Ferrari. That's not a good look."

"Corvette?" she asked like it was any better.

"No"

"Maserati?"

"Hell no."

"Oh my God. Oh, we have an Escalade."

"That's all you got that's normal?" he asked as he shook his head.

"Pretty much. Unless you want me to get one of my friends' cars, I might be able to get something inexpensive."

"We can take the Escalade, fuck it."

"Ok good."

Chapter 31

They got in and headed to the bus station. JC had the gun pointed to her ribs the whole time while she was driving. She had done everything he had told her to do so far and she seemed genuine enough but there was no way he was taking any chances. "I see you don't trust me," she said, glancing down at the gun that was poking her in the side.

"I don't trust anybody. Not just you. Don't take it personal," he told her with a slight shrug.

"Why are you wanted for murders?" she asked. Her voice didn't sound as scared as before. It sounded more curious now.

"Can you just drive and shut up please?" JC said. She was prying and asking too many questions, and he was getting impatient.

"I was just asking, damn man. Calm down."

"I am calm. You just drive."

Sandra turned up the radio and kept driving. She couldn't wait to get him out of her car. She was scared and confused at the same time. One minute they had been chilling and fucking and the next the damn police were beating down her door and her mom was telling her he was some kind of serial murderer. She didn't know what was going on but she didn't want any part of it. She just wanted to drop him off and go back home. Even though she was scared, the fact that he had a side to him that she hadn't known all along made her feel excited somehow. It made her wet thinking about having sex with a killer. That kind of turned her on while she was driving, and she shifted in her seat. Her friends would never believe her, but she planned on telling them one day.

When they arrived Sandra told him what to do and where to go. "Thanks. Get out of here," he told her.

"Bye, JC."

JC walked inside. The place was filthy. There were people everywhere, including bums and all. The place even stunk badly. "When is the next bus leaving?" JC asked an older lady that was walking with a cane.

"It's one about to leave in about 5 minutes right over there." She pointed to a bus a few yards away. "The guy have a extra seat he's trying to sell right now. I was going to buy it but it's going all the way to Las Vegas."

"Thanks."

Chapter 32

JC jogged over there and bought the ticket. He had got lucky with getting a ticket in the nick of time. He got into the bus and walked down the aisle trying to find somewhere to sit. It was packed like a sardine can and there were so many different smells that hit him as he was passing by, holding his backpack in front of him as he walked. A guy was running towards him holding an iPad that he had clearly just snatched from the dude he was sitting next to. He nearly ran JC over but JC caught him by the neck, putting him in a choke hold that caused him to drop the iPad. JC shoved him away and picked the iPad up. "Get yo' thieving ass out of here," he shouted at the guy.

The guy just looked at him and walked off the bus. "This yours?" JC asked the guy that was just now getting out of his seat to chase the guy. Of course he wouldn't have caught up with him, not at that pace.

"Yea. Thanks, man."

Everyone begin clapping on the bus and saluting JC. The guy grabbed his iPad, and told JC that a seat was available in the back right next to him where the other guy was just sitting. JC brought his stuff back there and sat down. "You knew him?" he asked the guy.

"Naw, we just was sitting next to each other and the nigga just snatched my shit, punched me on the side of the face, and took off running." He showed JC the bruise on the side of his jaw where the thief had caught him with his fist.

"Oh damn."

"Thanks to you though, I got my shit back. Good looking man. What's your name?"

"I'm JC. And you?"

"You can call me Dee. You from Atlanta or you just visiting?"

"Naw, I'm visiting. I'm from the Midwest. What about you? You from Atlanta?"

"Naw, I just came down here for a weekend to visit a couple friends. I'm born and raised in Vegas."

"How is Vegas? I never been there before. This is a first for me."

Dee looked at him with a surprised look on his face. "You never been to Vegas?"

JC shook his head no.

"Aw nigga you about to love Vegas. You not going to want to leave, I'm telling you."

JC smiled. "Why is that?"

"The women, the scenery, everything. Vegas is the shit."

"That's what I'm talking about."

Chapter 33

Soon, the bus was leaving and they were welcoming everyone aboard. JC let his seat slide back a little and started to relax after his ordeal as Dee was still talking to him animatedly. He could tell he wanted to be his friend bad. "My girl wanted to come with me but I told her to stay so she mad at me. When I get back I have to do something nice for her."

"What you have in mind?" JC asked, wondering what he was going to do. JC had to make up to quite a few women who were mad at him and he had experience in this kind of thing.

"I was thinking, maybe bring her some nice flowers, maybe some chocolates." He sounded usure.

"How long you been gone away from her?"

"6 days."

JC whistled and shook his head. "Aw naw, you gotta do more than that."

"Like what?" He seemed exasperated now that his idea had been shot down.

"You can do the flowers and the candy, but you need to make her feel like you miss her. You love her right?"

"Hell yea I love her. So you don't think flowers is saying all that? I don't normally do stuff like that, so I was thinking that might blow her mind."

"What do she like to do? She like food? She like going places?"

"Yea she like doing that too."

"Take her somewhere nice. Get dressed up and take her to have some fun. I never been to Vegas, but I can imagine that it has a lot of fun shit to do. Then after that, fuck her real good." JC grinned at the man like it had been obvious all along.

Dee laughed. "Ok, ok I got you. I'ma take her somewhere nice. She will like that. She always trying to get me to go places, but I be at the crib playing the game most of the time. She hates it, but she loves the shit out of me. We been together since middle school. I can honestly say she's probably the girl I'm going to marry, have kids with and spend the rest of my life with." The guy looked young but it was obvious he had fallen hard for his girl.

"That's what's up. Is she from Vegas too. How old is she?"

"19 like me and yep, born and raised." He motioned for him to wait a second and pulled out his phone. He started going through his phone and showing JC pictures of the two of them.

"Damn boy, you got you a baddie." JC took the phone and kept scrolling, looking through all the different pictures of the girl. His chick looked like Erica Mena in the face with a nice booty. "What is she mixed with?"

"She's Mexican and Cuban."

"She is gorgeous man for sure," JC told him approvingly. "Is this what they look like out there in Vegas?"

"Hell yea. It gets way better than this," he told JC. "It's foreign bitches everywhere bro. I'm telling you. How long you going to be in Vegas? We need to link up, I'll show you some shit. I got a few little side hoes and shit. You know I do my thing a little."

Chapter 34

JC laughed. "Shit, I don't have a limit to how long I'ma be in Vegas honestly. I'm just moving out here with my last man. I got like $900 to my name. I just broke up with my chick. She took a lot of my shit, and I'm just starting new."

"Oh shit, so you just moving to Vegas to try something new? You have anywhere to go? Like sleep?" Dee asked, looking concerned.

JC shook his head.

"Man, you can come stay with me until you get on your feet. I have a one bedroom. It's just me and my girl but you can have the couch."

"Shit that's cool. I'll try it out. It shouldn't take me too long to get on my feet." JC was relieved that he'd met Dee now.

"It's no rush. I don't fuck with many Vegas niggas, they weird. You seem cool though."

Hours later of riding, Dee couldn't shut up. He kept talking and talking about everything and nothing, and JC tried to keep listening to him. He wanted to keep on Dees's good side now that he was going to be crashing on his couch for a while, but listening to what he had to say was tough. The guy was a goldmine of information on life in Vegas.

Dee kept on talking. It was like he was super happy to be JC's friend. He was telling him everything he knew. JC felt cool just knowing he had a destination to go to. As he listened to Dee, JC noticed two chicks sitting to the right of them. One kept looking at him and smiling so he finally said something. "Where ya'll from?"

"Vegas and you?" one answered smiling.

"I'm from the Midwest. So, everybody is mixed or another race in Vegas? What are ya'll?"

They both giggled. "It's a melting pot there. I'm Asian and she's Blasian," she said, giggling.

"What's Blasian?"

"She's mixed with black and Asian. So blasian."

"Oh duh." They all laughed. JC liked the blasian one, so he focused more on her. She was the one that kept looking at him anyway, so he was fixed on her as he talked to the girls. "How old are ya'll?"

"We are both 20."

Chapter 35

D ee butted in and started talking as well, asking what the Asian girl was watching on her tablet. They got into a deep conversation about Lord Of The Rings which left the Blasian girl and JC talking to each other. "Aye let's switch seats for a little bit. You come over here and I go over there."

"Ok cool."

They switched spots and JC set next to the blasian girl. She couldn't stop smiling at him. "What's your name?"

"Roxi and you are?" she held her hand out to him and paused for a moment, waiting for him to shake it. JC looked at her hand and gave her a small shrug.

"JC and I'm not shaking your hand, you gotta give me a hug." He grinned at her and spread out his arms in a welcoming and familiar gesture.

She blushed and giggled as she moved around in her seat to face him and hug him from where she was sitting. As she hugged him, JC smelled the coconut scented shampoo in her hair.

"Damn you pretty and smell good," he commented with a hint of a wink that had her blushing a little harder.

"Thank you, you're so silly." She kept doing a little cute giggle that JC was liking.

"So, what was you doing in Atlanta?" he asked her, curious about what kind of person she was.

"Just doing some business. I come out here pretty often."

"What kind of business?"

"I'm trying to get bigger with making stripper outfits. So, I came out here to visit a couple strip clubs to see what kind of styles they are wearing. I can mimic it and sell them in Vegas one day." She seemed like the entrepreneurial and smart type, and JC liked that.

"That's cool. That seem like a good idea. So, you haven't started just yet?"

"No, not yet. Still just doing research."

"Have you made anything?"

"Yes, I have a few outfits that I've made, but I haven't like tried to sell them or anything."

"What you waiting for?"

She fluttered her eyes and let out a small sigh. "I don't know. It's kind of scary. I'm not sure if they are like, good enough."

"You gotta put it out there and see what happens." JC told her earnestly.

"I know, that's what my boyfriend says too. But I don't know. I'm not sure if I really want to do it or not."

"Well, you taking trips to Atlanta for it, so you must be somewhat serious."

"I have friends out in Atlanta too."

"And did you say boyfriend?" JC picked up on that immediately.

"Yes."

"You have one?"

"Yes, I do."

"How long ya'll been together?"

"Since high school off and on."

"Oh ok. Damn you got a boyfriend and you was smiling at me like how you was earlier?" JC grinned at her, watching for her reaction.

She giggled, and her cheeks pinkened. "I was not!"

Chapter 36

"You was. I thought I seen you wink at me too." JC tipped his head and gave her a lop-sided smile.

She couldn't stop laughing. "You are so funny. That is so not true JC, and you know it."

"So, I guess I'm seeing things now."

"I think so if you saying I was winking at you. I don't even know how to wink." She said as she started trying to wink. She was right, she couldn't wink at all. She ended up blinking or just tipping her eyebrows or pulling her cheeks up in a smile. JC thought it was cute seeing her try to wink, and when she finally gave up, they both started laughing. JC noticed her teeth were very pretty, next to perfect. They were pearly and perfectly white, like some girl out of a toothpaste ad. Her hair was black, long and curly, and she had full lips with mild cheek bones. When you looked at her from a distance, you knew she was pretty. But when you looked at her real close, she was definitely gorgeous.

"Why your boyfriend didn't come with you? He just let you get on this bus by yourself?" JC asked, wondering if the boyfriend was sitting somewhere else by any chance. He didn't want to get into any more trouble.

"He never comes. He's probably somewhere cheating again."

"Damn again? You say that like it happens often. A little too often."

"Sad to say but it does. He cheats, and I catch him all the time. And he still continues to cheat on me," she said as her mouth angled downwards.

"See, now I have to be your boyfriend. He not even treating you right."

She giggled and gave him a little sideways glance.

"I'm serious. You too pretty to be getting cheated on. He gotta go. You gone dump him or I got to beat his ass first?"

"What?" she burst out and laughter. "You are too funny. You are not going to fight my boyfriend."

JC laughed along with her. "If I beat him up, I can have you?"

She giggled and twirled a strand of her hair around her finger. "Oh my God, you are so funny." She started adjusting herself in her seat.

"I'm just saying."

"What are you saying?"

"If I beat your boyfriend up, are you going to be my girlfriend?"

"I don't even know how to answer that. I need help with that one. Natali!" She called out to her friend that was over in the other seat watching a movie with Dee.

"What's up?"

"What are you guys watching?"

"White chicks." She looked up from the movie and at JC and her friend.

"Oh my God. So, JC wants to know if he beats up my boyfriend, can me and him be together?"

Chapter 37

Natali laughed loudly and clapped her hands together approvingly. "That is such a good idea, JC. Yes, please beat him up. She needs a new boyfriend so bad."

They all burst out into laughter, making some of the passengers turn around and look at them.

"See, even she wants me to beat him up," JC said as he turned to look at Roxi.

"That's actually the only way he would probably stop coming around." She rolled her eyes.

"What you mean?"

"I've tried to dump him so many times. He just keeps coming back. Even if I met someone, he would probably scare them away. He just pops up all the time. Even when I'm mad at him." She sounded annoyed now that she recalled what her boyfriend kept doing.

"He not going to be able to do none of that anymore," he told her.

She giggled. "Whatever."

"Ya'll don't have any kids?" he asked, wondering if she had a bunch of kids back at home.

"No. He tries, but I always keep plan B's on deck. I do not want a baby by him."

"Why you still with the nigga? He black or white?"

"He's black. Your complexion. I'm not sure why I'm still with him."

JC gave her a sideways glance. "He got a big dick or something?"

She turned and looked at him, shocked that he had actually said that. "Oh my God, JC!" She hit him on his shoulder, biting back an embarrassed smile.

"What? I'm just trying to figure out what's keeping you," he retorted with a laugh.

"That may be one reason. He's a very nice size for sure." Her eyes went a little dazed at the mention of it.

"Ok and what else?"

"He's fun sometimes."

"He got a nice body?"

"Ummm, it's ok. He don't work out or anything."

"So he ain't got a body like this or nothing?" JC took off his shirt and showed her his body. His abs and pecks were looking like they were carved into his body. He knew he looked good and he wanted her to see.

"Jesus, put that up!" she said, blushing so hard that her whole face turned another color. Although she was telling him to get his shirt back on, the fact that she could barely drag her eyes away from his rock hard perfectly sculpted pecs and abs was encouraging. "Oh my God, you are hilarious. There is no shyness in you."

95

They were both laughing, and Natali and Dee were looking over there wondering what was going on. They peeked over at them, surprised at what sudden turn of events had made JC take off his shirt right there in the bus like that.

"He ain't got a body like that?"

"Hell no. Not even close. Oh my God. You have a nice body. I'm getting hot again. You too much," she said, looking over him again and squirming a little in her seat. "You might need to go back to your seat. I ain't ready for all this." She motioned with her hand, around his body then turned and started looking out the window.

Chapter 38

JC laughed and leaned in a little closer. "You liked what you saw or what?"

"I think any woman would like what she sees."

"I'm not talking about any woman. I'm talking about the one right here in front of me."

She was so embarrassed and her body was so hot that it felt like she was burning up at that point. "Yes. I like it...a lot. Maybe too much, that's why I want you to go back to your seat," she said sarcastically and they both laughed.

"Well it's all yours once I get rid of your boyfriend," he told her, whispering in her ear in a way that got her shivering with arousal.

Please get rid of him, she thought to herself. "We shall see."

"That's the only dude you ever been with?" he asked, wanting to know more about how experienced she was.

"Sexually no, he's the 5th. We broke up a couple times and I tried with other guys, but always end up back with him."

"Well we gonna get rid of him for good this time."

"Oh really?"

"Yes really."

She giggled. "I love the fact you are so confident. That's different. Vegas guys not like that. They are assholes. They are cocky assholes and disrespect women all the time, but still expect for us to give them everything they want, and when they want. Like, you just like, I'm going to beat your boyfriend up and take you from him." She giggled and looked at him again. "This may sound weird, but it's actually cute."

They both laughed.

"That's just how I am. If I see something I want, I'm willing to do whatever to get it."

"I love that. That's how people should be. Go after what you want. But wait, how do you know you want me? You barley even know me." She seemed to be more and more impressed with JC and attracted to him too, with every passing second.

"I want to get to know you. And what I've learned so far, I love. So If I have to move someone out my way to do that, that's what I'm going to do." JC's tone let her know he wasn't joking around. He was serious about it.

"We will see what happens. You seem cool. But all guys seem cool at first. Then once ya'll get what ya'll want, it be a different story." She had obviously had some really bad experiences with men but JC knew how to get around anything.

"What we want as far as what?"

"You know, some vagina."

"What if that's not what the guy is after?"

"Don't all guys want to just have sex with women?" She gave him a dubious look like he was crazy to tell her otherwise.

"No."

"Well what's your reason with me then?" She was surprised by everything he had told her so far and she wanted to know.

Chapter 39

"It's not sex, that's for sure. I'm looking at something much bigger than just that. I want to be married with kids, nice home, nice careers, good parenting and all that good stuff," he told her.

"And how can I be so sure?"

"My actions as long as you give me a chance."

"Well, you already said your beating my boyfriend up and taking me from him, so do I even have a choice?"

They both laughed, and JC knew that he had her in the bag now.

"Yea you right about that. Naw you don't have much of a choice, we almost locked in with that."

"Oh, so you just talking junk?"

"Naw I'm serious, I just still have to see you stand up and walk. Make sure you got a body and you not limping because you got a fake leg or something," he joked, with a grin spreading across his face.

She busted out and laughed so loud, it even scared JC. She was cracking up. "I don't have any of that." She stood up and turned around just a little bit, slightly gave him a peek of her back side. She had a nice body and a nice butt that stuck out and was the perfect size. It wasn't small, and it wasn't huge. It was just the right size.

"Damn baby, I see you got the body to go with your beautiful facial features. Yup you about to be my wife."

She giggled again and swatted at him, blushing at all his compliments.

"So serious, you too pretty to be riding this bus. You tripping."

"You know how many times I've heard that?"

"What?"

"That I'm too pretty to be riding this bus. What does that even mean? I think there is beautiful people on this bus," she said in such a sweet way.

"Since we boyfriend and girlfriend now, I'll fly you back to Atlanta when you want to go back."

She giggled and shook her head. "I'm scared of planes." She got in his face sarcastically.

"Train."

"Scared of trains." She crossed her arms and looked at him.

"We can drive."

"Oh, so you will take this drive with me?" she asked, surprised that he had offered.

"Hell yea, why not?"

"Because nobody else will, not even Natali."

They both started laughing. "Why not?"

"I don't know, some stuff she said about riding in cars too long or something. I don't know."

"Maybe she don't trust your driving skills."

She giggled and nodded in agreement. "That's actually a good point right there."

They both laughed again and she smiled at him. He gave her a teasing look.

Chapter 40

"**D**on't tell me you can't drive."

"I can. I guess I just scare people sometimes. I've never been in a accident or nothing though. I'm a safe driver. I'm holding you to that, with driving with me to Atlanta."

"Please hold me to it. I will drive anywhere on this planet with you girl," he said, jokingly.

She giggled. "You are so silly. It's cute though."

"So, when you gone text your ex and let him know it's over and you got new boyfriend?" he asked with a grin.

"Right now. Good idea." She started texting him which surprised JC. He hadn't expected her to give in so quick and break up with her boyfriend, but here she was doing it. He sat back to watch what was going to go down. As soon as she sent the breakup text, he started calling her. The phone kept ringing and she looked up at JC. "Oh my God, he's calling. What do I say?"

"The same thing you just texted him."

"Hello"

"What the fuck are you talking about?" A guy's voice shouted.

"I'm breaking up with you. I don't want to be in this relationship anymore."

"Why not?"

"Because I'm tired of going through stupid stuff. And you don't respect me at all," she said.

"What the fuck are you talking about? Are you having one of your little moments again?"

"No, I'm serious."

"What the fuck ever. Are you back yet?"

"No."

"We will see when you get back. I ain't got time for this shit."

"We won't see anything. I'm done. So please leave me alone." She looked at the phone screen and then at JC who looked at her. "He hung up in my face. Should I call back?"

"Naw, he will be ok."

"I can't believe I just did that for a guy I literally just met. I don't even know if the sex good or anything. Oh my God, what did I just do?" she whined, putting a hand over her face like she just might have made a mistake.

JC laughed. "I'll give you a sample soon, don't worry."

She looked at him and tilted her head with a slight smile. "You are too much. Do all the girls just dump their boyfriends for you?"

"No, you actually the first one that ever did that."

"Oh my gosh, are you serious? JC, you better not be playing mind games with me."

"Relax, give me a kiss."

Chapter 41

She froze up at that. He was so blunt, so direct. She wasn't used to that and she was hesitant for a moment because everything had happened so fast. She just sat there for a second and he leaned over and kissed her himself. "You not going to kiss me back?"

She fanned herself, "Ok it's getting hot in here again."

JC went in for another kiss, and this time she kissed him back. Her lips were nice and soft. "Ok, I can't believe I just did that. Oh my God."

JC laughed and squeezed her hand. "Relax, we go together now. Kissing gone be the new normal."

She started giggling and blushing. He had her going nonstop until they reached their first stop which was for some food. JC bought her food, although she was wrestling him trying to buy him food. Finally, she let him. That was something that she wasn't really used to, a guy treating her right. JC felt bad that she'd been stuck with guys who didn't even buy her some lunch. They spent hours together joking and playing and getting to know each other, and Roxi felt so safe with him. She had had her doubts breaking up with her controlling boyfriend for a guy she just met on the bus, but as she got to know JC better, she felt more and more comfortable with him. They laughed at each other's jokes which was another thing she wasn't used to. Her ex always called her stupid and corny but JC always laughed at her jokes even if they weren't funny. She saw what she had been missing, someone who put an effort into making her feel good and special. If he seen she was even attempting to tell a joke, he was laughing at her. He wanted her to feel comfortable with him. He liked her but he also needed her. When he first got on the bus, he didn't know what he was going to Vegas for, now he was feeling like he had a purpose again. He was going to try to enjoy himself until things cooled down. Between crashing at Dee's place and having Roxi around, he felt like he had some solid ground under his feet again even though he was headed to a brand-new city he'd never set foot in.

The bus drive seemed like forever, but he needed this time to get to know Roxi and Dee more. They laughed, talked and exchanged stories, and really got to know each other. Not to mention it was getting hot and heavy with Roxi. By the second night on the bus ride, JC and Roxi were tongue kissing and feeling on each other under her blanket. "So when was you going to tell me, you had all this," she asked while rubbing his dick up and down through his pants.

"I wasn't going to tell you. You woulda found out eventually." JC grinned at her.

"This a lot."

"Too much for you?"

"Naw, I will be ok. This a lot though. Something I would have to get used to." She sounded like she was a bit nervous but up for the challenge.

"How you know you gone be ok? You had a dick this size before?"

"No, I haven't. This will be for sure, the biggest," she said, giggling. She felt it again, tracing its outline as it snaked inside his pants. "By far."

The next stop, they stopped at a truck spot. "This is where we can actually take showers at."

Chapter 42

A shower sounded really good to JC, but he wasn't so sure about the condition of the spot.

"Is it clean?" he asked, glancing out of the window.

"Yes, at this place it is. Sometimes they stop at ran down locations, but this is a good location. They are just more expensive," Roxi explained.

"They cost?"

"Yea, just $15. It's a nice size private room."

JC was going to ask to come in her room with her, but since it had been so long since either of them showered, he was going to his own. They were at the stop for a couple hours, and of course everyone didn't get to take a shower or even try to take one. JC managed to take a nice long shower and freshen up. When he was done, he stepped outside and saw that Roxi had finished her shower too. They followed each other back to the bus. JC was liking her a lot at that point. She was about 5ft7 and had nice curves. Very pretty in the face, and he couldn't wait to get inside her. He had talked to Dee about her and Dee was telling him he shoulda waited until he got to Vegas before he said he was her boyfriend, because there are so many beautiful women, but JC couldn't wait. He got what Dee was saying but he had already made up his mind about Roxi. He had never had even an Asian girl, and this one was Blasian; he wasn't about to miss out on her. He didn't care about her not having much money. He actually liked her. She was far from a street girl, and that's what he felt like he needed right now to keep him calm. But he told Dee they were still going to have some fun with the ladies. JC felt like he could tell Roxi anything and she would believe it. And so far he was right. She didn't have any reason to not believe his words. She was really stuck on him and impressed by everything he did. It was obvious she was starved for affection, and after being stuck with a guy like her ex-boyfriend, she was feeling free.

It had been days since they had been on the bus and they had finally made it to Vegas. JC's lips were dry due to all the kissing Roxi kept doing. It was like she had fallen in love on the bus ride. She didn't even want him to go back to his regular seat. She insisted that he stay in the one next to her so she could keep kissing and cuddling with him. As they got off the bus, Dee's girlfriend was there to pick them up. She ran up to him and hugged and kissed him. "Baby I miss you so so much. Vegas is not the same without you. I was so bored," she said, kissing him all over his face. JC could tell they were for sure in love.

Chapter 43

"Hey this my cousin JC. JC this is Akira. He's going to be staying with us for a little while," he told her, introducing them to each other.

JC put out his hand for her to shake it. She did and smiled. "Hi cousin JC."

"How you doing?"

"I'm doing better now, now that he's back home. Come on, let's go. Y'all hungry?"

She was nicer than JC expected. Roxi wanted him to go with her, but JC told her they will see each other soon. She texted him all the way until he got to Dee's house.

Roxi: I miss you already. I smell like you too.

JC: I miss you too. Let me get a small feel for being in Vegas then we will link.

Roxi: You know I leave the day after tomorrow to go to California. So, will it be before that? I hope so. I really want to see you.

JC: Damn I forgot about that. I may come over later then.

Roxi: Please do, I'll be waiting for you.

JC: That just sounded so sexy, my dick jumped.

Roxi: LMAOOOOOOOO!!! You are so funny. I can't wait to see you.

JC: See you soon baby.

They drove JC down to the strip just to give him a taste of Vegas. Everything he saw dazzled him. It was nothing like Atlanta. All the sounds and lights and people made him feel excited just looking at it all. He felt like a little kid looking at all the fine architecture. Everything just looked so big and exciting. People were out, walking around, smiling, taking pictures, dancing, riding bikes, and everything you could think of. JC had never seen or experienced anything like this before. It made him feel different. He didn't feel like the same guy he was before. This was a fresh new start right here and all the adventure he could want. He didn't know that there was this much more to life. All he had known was Michigan, but Vegas was something different. The whole vibe was on another level. He didn't have a worry in the world. There were so many people walking around and driving around, he knew in his heart, he could actually live here and be free again. It seemed like Vegas was meant for him. It wasn't an accident that he'd caught that bus out here, it was meant to be. He was willing to bet on it. They stayed out until 10pm that night. Roxi kept blowing him up telling him how she missed him and still hoped to get to see him. Dee was right, she was clingy, but since he liked her, he didn't mind at all. He told Dee and his girl to drop him off over Roxi's house for the night and that he was going to let them get their privacy. They drove up to Roxi's place and dropped him off by the driveway. It was dark but he could see the front door opening.

Chapter 44

As he walked to Roxi's door, she was standing there waiting for him in some sexy night clothes. The pink leggings were hugging her perfect body to show off all her curves, and the sports bra she wore made her tits look perfect. She had pulled her hair back into a messy bun on top of her head.

"Damn, girl you so fine." He gave her a hug and kiss and took a step back to admire her.

"Aww you are to sweet. Ok follow me. This is the living room, kitchen, dining room and my room is upstairs." They walked upstairs. "This is my room, me and you can share it whenever you want to," she said, giggling.

She had a nice size room, with a queen size bed, a dresser and a tv that sat on top of her dresser, "Make yourself comfy, and I'll get you whatever you want."

"First I want to get in the shower, then we can relax. You don't have any liquor or nothing?"

"You're a drinker?"

"Sometimes, not often."

"What you like? They have plenty downstairs. I can go get you some, or I can go to the store and pick some up if we don't have what you want."

"I like dark."

"Like?"

"Henny, Dulce."

"Ok I know we don't have any of that down there. What about Jack or Jameson?"

"Jack will do. That's cool. With some ice. While you get that, I'm getting in the shower. Where's the towels?"

"I got you baby, one second."

She got everything ready for him, "Next time, if you tell me before you get here, I would have everything ready for you."

"It's ok, baby. Thank you."

"You so welcome." She smiled at him and handed him all the towels and things.

JC walked in the bathroom and began stripping his clothes off. Roxi was a sweetheart, and she was just getting nicer and nicer. He had a good feeling about her. But he couldn't get money off his mind. He needed to get some money. He needed clothes and a lot of other things. He took himself a long hot, comfortable shower and thought about everything then tried to clear his mind so he could be in the moment while he was in Vegas for the first time. He didn't want to think about everything he'd left behind. That would only hang a dark cloud over his time in the new city. He was happy that he made the move, and he hadn't even seen much just yet.

Chapter 45

"When he came out, he just had on his boxer briefs and some basketball shorts on, no shirt. "Baby you know I'm about to be all over your sexy body. I don't know why you doing this to yourself," she said while sitting on the bed with her arms wide open. She looked like she was excited to get her hands on him. She hadn't been able to get her hands all over him like she wanted to on the bus with it being in public and all. But now, he could tell by the look in her eyes that she was hungry for him.

He smiled, "It's all for you. I want you to be all over this body."

"Ok, I don't want to hear anything about me being too clingy and all that. You just gave me permission."

JC laughed and nodded, "I sure did. I hope I don't regret it."

She dropped her mouth wide open, looking confused by what he had just said. "What does that mean?"

"I'm just kidding boo. Come here."

She came right to him and wrapped her hands around his body and gave him some sexy, wet kisses. "I just love your kisses so much. Your lips is so soft."

"Yours are too." They continued to kiss as she fell back slowly on the bed with him being on top of her, his body weight pushing her down into the mattress. She wanted him badly and couldn't hide it.

"You get my drink baby?" he asked in between kisses.

"Yes, it's on the dresser behind you."

"You bring a glass?"

"Yes baby," she said still trying to kiss him and get him to have sex with her. She was so impatient, but JC wanted to take his time and savor it.

"You drinking with me?"

"I don't drink, baby, sorry."

"It's ok, it's ok," he said, pecking her on her lips over and over. "You so pretty Roxi, damn."

"You really think so?" she asked, looking him in his eyes, and kissing him again and again.

"Hell yea," he said as he continued to kiss her, tongue kissing her for a little longer then pulling back, to make himself a drink.

"Baby, your body, is so sexy," she told him as she admired him, standing up fixing himself a drink. She was eyeing his dick print that was buldging through his shorts. She was having a hard time controlling herself. She wanted him but she didn't want to get demanding or pushy. In his head, he was putting Roxi at the top of the list, as far as the prettiest girl he ever dealt with. He wanted to keep her and keep her safe. From the talk on the bus, she said her mom and aunts are very loyal women and that's how she was raised. He liked that and hoped that it was true. Although his motto was to not trust, he was thinking about letting his guard down with this one. She seemed pretty harmless and sweet. He didn't trust women` not to screw him over. But Roxi wasn't like that. She was falling in love and ready to do anything he wanted.

"Thank you," he said, as he winked at her.

"Oh my God, did you just wink at me? Do it again. I can't do it for nothing in this world."

Chapter 46

She seemed to get a lot of laughs out of his winks, and she loved it when he winked at her.

He laughed as he took a drink, and winked at her again. She smiled again and couldn't wait to get her hands on him. He saw it all in her face. She was so into him, but he was into her as well. He sat right next to her, and she started rubbing his shoulders. She let her fingers run into his muscles and melt the tension right out of his shoulders. "Oh, I give great massages too, just to let you know."

"Good. I love massages and it's been a while since I got one." JC relaxed under her hands and let her massage his tight muscles.

"You can have one anytime you want."

They set back and talked while she snuggled under him. She wanted him so bad she didn't know what to do. Once he finished his drink and got a little buzz going, he started kissing her again which she had been waiting for. She kissed him back eagerly. She climbed on top of him almost immediately, straddling his hips with her nice, soft thighs. They kissed and kissed as both of their breathing got heavier. When she felt his dick hardening and jumping underneath her, she let out a little moan of want. JC slid her leggings down and she eased one leg out. She didn't even bother taking them all the way off. Their lips were locked, and Roxi leaned over as she wanted him to get on top of her. He followed her lead, and her hands stripped his shorts down, revealing his long, black, hard dick. She broke the kiss long enough to get an eyeful of his dick and that seemed to drive her crazy.

As they were still tongue wrestling, she grabbed his dick softly and started rubbing the head of it between her pussy lips, making herself wetter than she already was. "Be gentle with me, baby," she whispered as she continued to kiss him, her breath coming in soft pants as she whined at the sensation of his tip grazing her clit.

"I got you, baby," he said as he grabbed his dick and started easing inside her, inch by inch. "I got you baby," he whispered again as he watched her eyes roll while he entered her slowly. She let out a long moan, throwing her head back as she savored the feeling of his dick filling her up. She received him very well, but JC knew she felt every inch of him. He eased slowly in and out of her, going as slow as possible. "Damn, you feel so good," he said, as their lips were slightly touching. He stroked her for minutes as she held onto the back of his neck, kissing him nonstop. She was moaning very low.

"You ok, baby?" he asked, purring deep into her ear.

Her head went up and down with a smile on her face. "Yes," she whispered, with two wet marks at the crack of both of her eyes. "It's so good. I don't wanna be too loud and have my roommates hear me."

Chapter 47

❝Turn your tv up a little more. Then you can relax." He pulled his dick out of her. It was shiny and wet, and it had thick, clear creamy fluid on it. "You came?"

She giggled, "I came before you was even inside me, yes."

That made JC smile. She was so thirsty for him and wanted him so much.

"Damn." He stood there butt ass naked and turned up the tv. His shaft was sticking straight out barley moving. He was so hard now, he wanted to get his dick wet again and cum inside her. He soon was climbing back on top of her and putting his dick back inside. It went in a lot easier this time. She was so wet, and he managed to slide it in smoothly. He started long stroking her as she was doing her best to take all of him.

"Baby, baby, yes, yes, yes," she gasped loudly in between each stroke. He was stroking her so perfect; it wasn't too hard or soft. "Yes, oh my God, JC, yes baby," she moaned as she reached for his head to kiss him, sticking her tongue all in his mouth. "I'm cumming baby, yes," she moaned and locked lips with him again. He kept stroking her nonstop and soon she was shaking and cumming while JC was still stroking her slowly. She shuddered with pleasure and her pussy spasmed as she came hard, her whole body heating up and shivering as waves of pleasure washed over her.

She was in heaven as he continued to stroke her. The places he was going inside her, had her losing her train of thought. His arms were so cut and strong, his abs were rocking with every stroke and sweat was starting to drip from his chin. She kissed him and held him deep inside her, and he started to dig. "Baby!" she moaned louder, scratching his back and holding on to his strong body. "Baby...Baby....Baby!" she moaned as he pumped inside her, deeply. She felt like his dick was in control of her body and hitting all the right spots. She moaned every time he hit the right spot, and her hips moved on their own accord, grinding down on him in time with each thrust to take him deeper.

"That feels good?" he whispered in between heavy breathing.

"Yes! Baby yes!" she moaned as her mouth was wide open and she took his strokes. It seemed like it lasted forever. JC thrusted into her in a fast and deep rhythm as she moaned underneath him, begging for more.

"I'm cumming," he whispered as his body was barley moving. His thrusts were slow and sloppy now that he was right on the edge. He started rocking from left to right, as his sperm shot out of his dick into her wetness. It felt like he had released gallons. The hot wet liquid spurted into her in a steady stream. "This pussy so good," he told her and they started back kissing while he laid on top of her. She was so affectionate. He wasn't really used to it, but he was actually enjoying it. She was drop dead gorgeous and for her to be into him like she was, it turned him on. He was so happy that he met her.

Chapter 48

"It's yours, baby. It's all yours, baby," she moaned. She felt his dick throbbing inside her as it finally started to soften up. "I love your lips so much," she said, kissing him three times again before he pulled out of her and got up and went in the bathroom. "I don't think I can move, you stretched me out. I know I'm going to be sore."

"You'll be ok."

"We'll see." She turned over and put her legs together and just admired JC as he was washing his dick off. Her pussy felt like it was wide open. "I'm not on birth control, just letting you know that."

"Didn't we already have this conversation on the bus, that we was making babies?" JC told her with a grin.

The smile that came across her face was priceless. She was excited, and touched that he wanted all that with her. "That's true."

"You thought I was playing?"

"Let's just say, I'm glad you are keeping your word. That means a lot to me." She smiled at him softly, still watching him with pure adoration on her face.

"Always."

He came back and got in the bed and she was all over him, rubbing his chest and abs as he changed channels on the tv, looking for something to watch. He looked down at her and she must've felt him, because she looked up, and he gave her a kiss on the lips.

The next morning JC woke up and Roxi was still knocked out. He got up and used the bathroom and started getting dress. Dee had texted him to make sure he was good. He texted him back and told him that he could come pick him up. He then kissed Roxi on the cheek, "Baby I'm about to leave in a second. You need anything?"

She turned a little and opened her eyes. "No, baby. Thanks. When are you coming back?"

"Maybe later."

She opened her arms and puckered her lips up as he kissed her. "I told you I would be sore. You stretched me out," she said as she tried to move. She was trying to get up but her legs were still like jelly and aching after what he'd given her last night.

"Hold on," he said, as he dropped his stuff. He made her lay back while he kissed and licked on her pussy until he made her cum then she raised up and tongue kissed her juices from his lips. "You are too much. Are you trying to make me fall in love with you?"

"Yep."

Chapter 49

S he smiled and he was out the door. Dee had been waiting for him, but as he was walking down the stairs he saw Natali at the bottom. "Oh my God, where's Roxi, Larry just pulled up."

"Who his Larry?"

"Her boyfriend, well her ex. Roxi!" she yelled, panicking.

"What!"

"Larry is outside," she said, running up the stairs.

Roxi didn't move. She didn't seem to care. "Leave him outside. I told him it was over."

"At least get up, they are going to fight. You know how Larry is." Natali got her up. She was sore and could not walk regularly. By the time she got down the stairs, JC had already knocked him out, even before Dee went to get out of the car to help. Roxi stared at Larry who was flat on his face.

"Oh my God, what happened?"

"He was being disrespectful. I told him to leave. He didn't listen."

The girls ran over to Larry, and he was on the concrete in the drive way snoring with a swollen eye. "Oh my God. Is he sleeping?" Roxi asked, confused.

"He'll wake back up in a little bit. Come give me a kiss," JC told her. She ran over to him and hugged and kissed him. "Now you for sure my girlfriend. I told you I was gone beat his ass."

She smiled and shook her head and went back into the house. JC and Dee got in the car and drove off.

"Who the fuck was that?" Dee asked.

"Her boyfriend. Well ex-boyfriend. I told that nigga to stand down and get the fuck on, but he thought he was tough since he was bigger than me."

"Yea I was just about to get out and help you with that nigga, but that first punch knocked his ass right out."

They both started laughing.

"I ain't even know I was gone knock him out with the first one, I knew he was gone with the second one though. But he didn't last that long."

They both laughed again and JC's phone rang. It was Roxi. "Hello."

"Can you come back? He's about to kick my door down." She sounded scared, and JC was suddenly filled with anger.

"Turn around and go back," JC said to Dee. He turned around in the middle of the streets and headed back.

"On my way. Just stay inside. I'm coming."

125

"I don't understand why he just won't leave me alone. I told him I was completely done this time. I guess breaking up so much in the past, he didn't take it serious."

"I'm here. Hold on." JC stepped out the car and Larry was kicking the door. He was tall and was a solid 260. "Aye man, what the fuck wrong with you? You want me to knock your ass out again?"

Chapter 50

"Fuck you. I didn't see it coming. Try that shit again," Larry growled, ready to fight.

Dee got out, as he saw Larry coming off the porch towards JC.

"Oh y'all gone jump me?" he asked, stepping back. He was on his guard now.

"Hell yea," Dee said.

"Naw, don't jump in. Matter fact, you can get back in the car," JC said, taking off his shirt.

All the girls were looking out the window, including Roxi. They all turned and looked at Roxi when JC shirt came off. "Yes, that's my man. He need to put that back on," she said as she hit the window as if he could hear her. All the girls laughed and Roxi smiled proudly, enjoying the fact that everyone could see that JC was hers and that he was fighting for her.

Once Dee got in the car, JC and Larry were face to face. Larry started swinging first, but JC ducked all his punches, and caught him clean, two times with a left and a right, dropping him. Larry's legs buckled and he fell in a squat first then on his back. JC came and stood over him, looking down at him. "Nigga," he said as he punched him with a right, "she said," he punched him with a left, "she don't," he said as he punched him with a right and Dee was pulling him off. He was losing control and it took some effort to get him away and off Larry who was near unconscious.

"Bro, chill. You gone kill him," Dee said as he dragged JC away.

Larry's face was swollen, his nose and mouth were bleeding. JC walked back and got in the car and picked up his phone. Roxi was still holding. "Hello."

"Yes. Are you ok?" she asked. "You just kicked his ass." All her roommates were in the background yelling, and happy about him finally getting beat up. Larry was usually the one doing the beating up, but it was like he didn't have a chance with JC. Everyone was cheering for JC.

JC laughed. "Yea I'm good. Is he leaving?"

"Yes, he's getting in his car right now. I can't believe you just did that. I'm like over here shaking right now. I was so scared. Oh my God, JC."

JC laughed. "It's ok. I'm sure he's going to leave you alone. We will see what happens."

"I'm so happy to be done with him. He was such a bully. He used to come here, eat all my roommates' snacks, their food, and drink up everything. Then I be stuck having to pay for it all. I'm so happy you did that JC. That's so cool," Roxi told him.

JC was just listening. He had her on speaker phone. Dee was laughing in silence how much Roxi was reacting.

Chapter 51

"He was such a doosh bag," she said. He could tell she was relieved. She didn't know how to keep him away. He had already beat one of her other guy friends up, and a couple of her roommates' boyfriends. She would have left him for good a long time ago if there had been someone to keep him away and protect her like JC had.

"So, what you about to do?"

"I think I'm going to take a hot bath, I'm sore," she said, giggling, "Like really sore."

"Aww baby, yea soak that thang for a lil' while, and let me know when you ready for me to go back in."

She giggled and whispered, "I know where it can go."

"Where."

"My mouth."

"That will work too, I'ma get with you later."

"I'll be waiting."

"Ok baby, talk to you later."

He hung up. "Man, you going to have these Vegas girls in love with you, going crazy."

"Why you say that?"

"Because, you can fight, nice body, no homo, you sweet talking and all that. These guys out here don't be doing all that. You know, it's pimps out here? This like the capital of chicks tricking."

"Oh, I ain't know that."

"Hell yea. I can tell your girl is not like that though. But most of these girls selling pussy for sure. It's a lot of money out here. Look around. What kind of cars you see that you didn't see in the Midwest?"

"Shit, all the foreign, exotics and all that shit."

"Man you gone see a Lambo on damn near every street you get on."

They laughed.

"You going to like Vegas. I'm telling you. Like what you just did, if you beat up a stripper boyfriend, she and all the other strippers going to be tryna pay you. They need that protection. Now don't get it twisted, these pimps will shoot your ass over their bitch. But just having the mentality you have, you going to be good."

"We will see. I'm tryna meet some other chicks. What dating site or social media the chicks be on out here?"

"Everything, Facebook, Snapchat, Instagram. But you can meet some chicks on Tinder too."

"What the fuck is that?"

"A dating app, where you sign up. It's free. But you can just swipe left or right to who you like or don't like. If they swipe the same way as you, like them liking you, then it's a match and now you can message her or she can message you."

"Oh you can't just message anyone on there?"

"Naw, it have to be a match."

"Man where I come from, niggas and bitches look down on people on dating apps."

"Why?"

"They look at it as being desperate or thirsty."

"You lived in a small town?"

"Yea why?"

"That's what that sounds like. Man out west, when I travel to Cali, AZ or wherever, everyone use dating apps, ain't nothing wrong with that. I be sneaking on there sometimes. My girl, be tripping though, so I can't do much."

JC laughed. As he looked down at his cell phone. Roxi was texting him.

Chapter 52

Roxi: I really hope you come back later.

JC: I will.

*R*oxi: *Not only me now, but my roommates think you are so cute and so cool. They all are happy Larry finally got beat up.*

JC: Lol

Roxi: lol I know right....Kisses, see you later.

"So I'm guessing you hit that right?" Dee asked, with a smile on his face.

"For sure," JC responded with a slight grin. "Back to this Tinder shit. You gotta get me set up with that shit."

"I got you. I'll get you set up when we get back to the crib. Actually, I'ma let my girl set you up, so she won't think I'm trying to be sneaky or something. Oh shit, her friend going to be coming over. She sexy too. You need to hit that too."

"What she look like?"

"Man she Armenian and white with an accent. She look like the singer Shakira to me. And she got a fat ass."

JC laughed. "We'll see. She got some money?"

Dee laughed. "She a waitress at one of the Casinos. That's another thing you going to realize. A lot of chicks here, waitress. But they make pretty good money off their tips. Like $300-$400 a night. And then when we have a big event, like the one, next weekend, they make more. We hitting the strip that weekend, Mayweather got a fight going on. It's going to be jumping. People from all over the world gone be in this bitch. All the hoes be fucking too. Pussy everywhere," he said, smiling.

JC laughed, Dee was excited. But he had no idea JC didn't really care about the pussy much. He was more worried about the money. "What you do for work? Like how you be getting money and shit?"

"Honestly, I be doing a little of everything."

"Like?"

"Selling a lil weed, credit card scams, shit like that. I be on the dark web a lot."

"What's on the dark web? I heard about it, but I ain't never been on it or nothing."

"Man, I den met all type of people on there that do all kinds of shit. They can get anything."

"I hear you. But like what?"

"You know Identity theft is like the biggest crime right now and growing. I can get social security cards, any state id's, birth certificate, nigga everything."

"Damn, how much something like that be costing?"

"It ranges. It depends how good you want it done. I know a guy that can get you some authentic shit. He lives right here in Vegas. He's Russian, nigga he can give you a

133

whole new everything, and it will pop up in the system, all that. He got plugs. Plus, he got a surgeon that he can change your face too." Dee started laughing.

"How much? Not for the face thing."

"I'll call him right now. We only talk through these encrypted apps." Dee dialed his number.

Chapter 53

"Hello."

"Hey how much you charge to change a person whole identity with everything he needs?"

"$25,000. My shit authentic, you know that. If you want, you can go pay $2,000 for some shit, that may last you a few years. But what I do, last forever."

"Ok cool. And how much for the face surgery?"

"You talking about $50,000 and up."

"Ok, I'll let him know, and get back with you when I hear something."

"Ok thanks buddy, take care."

"$25,000 for some real shit that will pass anywhere."

"I think I'ma get that," JC said.

"You want a new identity?"

"Yea, just to have though."

"That's cool."

"You have to show me how to use that app, that way I can call him up when I need him."

"Fasho, I got you."

They were soon walking into Dee's place. "Akira! You dressed?"

"Yes, I am," she said, peeking of out the bathroom while brushing her teeth. She waved when she saw JC.

"You be playing Madden?"

"Hell naw, but I'll play though," JC said as he set on the couch. Dee sat on the other sofa and started hooking the game up.

"I be whopping niggas ass in this Madden, this another thing I be doing to get money. Betting on this shit."

JC laughed, "Damn that's crazy. How much you be making?"

"I might play for about $50 a game. Sometimes $100. Akira what time Sara coming over?"

"About 5 o'clock."

"I want her to meet JC. We should all kick back and play some spades and have some drinks."

"That's cool. I'll ask her and see what she says. I'm sure she going to want to see him first Dee. You know how she is."

"I'll ask her when she get here," Dee said, smiling. "It's just to chill."

"Right, Akira, what you on over there?" JC butted in.

Akira giggled. "I just figured you was like any other guy, trying to get with her or something."

"Naw I just want some good company that's all. I ain't looking for nothing. I'm in Vegas, I'm trying to have fun."

"You will, don't worry."

"Can you set him up one of those Tinder pages?"

"Yea I can do that."

They chilled most of the day and told JC a lot about Vegas while they were playing each other in the game. Akira was sitting right there watching. She set up JC page and posted four pictures of him on there. Then she showed him how to use it. Showing him how to swipe right and left. The app was pretty easy to use, so easy, she taught him while he was playing a video game. JC was excited, and he saw some very attractive picks on there that he planned to get to after he met Sara.

"I'm going to go jump in the shower right fast," JC said, as he looked at the time and noticed that it was already 4 o'clock.

He jumped in the shower and got himself together. Vegas was a different vibe. He loved it so far, and he liked the people he was meeting. They didn't seem like they had any motive or anything. They just seemed genuine to him.

Chapter 54

Once he was done showering, he put on some grey sweats, a t-shirt and some sneakers. He thought about growing all his hair back since he was in Vegas.

"Dee went to go get some food for us," Akira said, as she eyed JC once he stepped out the bathroom.

"Ok that's cool." JC said as he got his stuff together and sat down on the couch. Roxi had sent him a text message.

Roxi: Hey, what you doing?

JC: Visiting some family. What you doing?

Roxi: Nothing. Guess who called?

JC: Larry.

Roxi: Yes.

JC: What he say?

Roxi: Oh my God, where do I start? He said so much. He was saying how he loves me and want to be with me and he is sorry for how he treated me but I'm like it's over. I just want you to leave me alone.

JC: lol he's funny smh.

Roxi: I know right, he dogged me. I'm like, I have someone new, that appreciates me and respects me. Kick rocks.

JC: Good.

Roxi: He was like he wants a rematch. lol I'm like, you need to sit down, and not get yourself embarrassed anymore.

JC: SMH, yes, he better move on.

Roxi: He so mad. I think it's so funny. Ugh, never again. I never want to deal with a person like that ever in my life.

JC: No worries, you stuck with me, for life now. And I'm not like that at all.

Roxi: I like when you say stuff to me like that.

He then sent her a blowing a kiss emoji. "So how long you out here for?" Akira asked.

"I'll be here for a while."

"You planning on like living in Vegas?"

"Yea, that's the plan. Just gotta get a few things together first. Get a feel for where I'm at. Where I come from, it's not as busy like here. Like earlier for example, it was morning and people was out walking, like shit moving down here like crazy. All the gas stations and everything is busy."

"Oh yea, for sure. Vegas is a busy city. This city never sleeps. People are everywhere. But like in a good way. It's not like a New York where it's congested and super crowded."

"Right, it's cool. I like it so far. So, we will see what happens."

"I think you going to like it a lot."

"So far it's looking good," he said before he read Roxi's next text.

Chapter 55

*R*oxi: *You're so sweet. So, I'm going to go get my routine petty and Manny and I'll call you or text you later. I hope you're still coming later.*

JC: Ok cool. Yes, I'll let you know if something change. It is looking like the family trying to hang out tonight though. They haven't seen me in years, so you know how that is.

Roxi: Oh no, I'm not going to get in the middle of that. We will get together when I come back no problem.

JC: Ok that's cool. Send me some pictures.

Roxi: What kind?

JC: My eyes-only pictures.

Roxi: JC! It's too soon for that. Not yet.

JC: I just nutted all in you. How is it too soon for some exclusive pictures?

Roxi: Lol @ the way you said that. You're so funny. I guess you do have a point there. Ok, maybe one or two. What color do you like?

JC: On you, I think you going to be sexy in any color.

Roxi: Awww, ok, I'll take one for you.

JC: Two.

Roxi: lmbo okkkk!

Dee soon was walking in the door with the food. He had brought back some chicken and fries. "Good looking bro, what I owe you?" JC asked.

"You good bro, no worries."

They all sat down and ate and by the time they were done, Sara was walking in. She was pretty and she really did look like a Shakira. JC instantly was able to tell from the front that she had a big booty. Her hips were curvy, she kept her body up, no stomach, with some big tits. She spoke to everyone and gave everyone hugs including JC then they sat down and talked. After about an hour of interacting, Dee spoke up. "So what's up, y'all going to chill with us tonight?"

JC and Sara had already been hitting it off. She was a pretty girl with a very attractive body, but JC learned from talking to her that she didn't have any money. He was looking for a chick with some money. Sara still lived with her mom and even got money from her mom sometimes. The only thing that kept him from going off to go with Roxi, was that Sara was pretty, foreign, with a fat ass. Plus, her accent was sexy. He had caught her checking him out every time he stood up. He also caught her and Akira texting back and forth, so he knew he had her. She got up often to show her body off to him, trying her best to entice him. The music was playing pretty loud but not too loud, and Sara and Akira were up dancing, twerking and popping their booties. JC noticed Akira could dance really good and he caught her a few times, glancing at him from the corner of her eye.

Chapter 56

A couple hours later, everyone had been drinking, and was tipsy. Dee was playing the game while Sara and JC talked. Akira kept twerking in front of him, trying to get his attention but he still continued to play the game, smiling.

"So how long you going to be out here in Las Vegas?" Sara asked, sipping on her vodka.

"A lil' minute. We gonna have to link up and do something before I go."

"For sure. I agree. Here, give me your number." She passed him her phone and he dialed his number in there. He was eyeing her thighs in the white pants she was wearing while she was moving sexy to the beat of the music.

"I see you like to party."

"Hell yea man, love to party. I'm young and free, so why not have fun, you know?"

"I feel you. You don't have any kids?"

"No and I don't want any. That's why I have this protection in my arm, you know."

"So, I can nut in you and have no worries?"

"Oh my God!" she yelled standing up, giggling, running over to Akira and telling her. Akira was still in her own world, dancing by herself while Dee was playing the video game. She soon came back over smiling, and still red in the face. "You are so crazy. The stuff you say, have me cracking up. You're not being from here is obvious."

"I said something wrong?"

"No, no not that. Nevermind."

"You still ain't answer my question."

She giggled again. "Yes, you can nut in me and not have to worry about nothing." Her face became bright red as she sipped her drink and crossed her legs.

"Good."

"You know how to dance?" she said.

"Nope."

"Aww, you suck."

JC looked down at his phone as Roxi was texting him. There were two pictures she sent. She had on a two-piece lime green lingerie outfit. She took the picture standing up and turned to the side, showing her booty. And the other one, was her stretching her arm to take a picture of her butt, bent over. JC could tell she was an amateur, but it wasn't anything he couldn't fix.

JC: Damn baby, you so sexy. That body so perfect. I love it.

Roxi: Aww you're so sweet. You think my body really perfect?

JC: Yes baby. Maintain that size right there for me.

Roxi: Anything for you baby.

JC: I like that.

Roxi: I like you.

JC: I like you back.

"Because I can't dance? You can dance for me, stand up and dance in front of me," he said, and surprisingly she did, she started swaying her hips then turning around, bouncing her ass. He started slapping it and she looked back.

"I didn't say you can touch it."

"Shit, I couldn't help it. It's soft too, this all you? Or you got some work done?"

"All me boo boo. All natural," she said as she kept dancing for him.

Chapter 57

Akira was still in her zone as the music blared through the speakers. Sara twerked slowly off the song that was playing, and it was turning JC on. Although Roxi was still texting, he had his eyes on Sara's booty. He grabbed her belt loop and pulled her back, making her drop on his lap. She started moving while her hands were on her knees, and JC's dick was bulging through his sweatpants. She felt it and wasn't stopping. "Somebody's up," she said as she was working her hips.

"Thanks to you." He held her waist and directed her hips.

"What you going to do about it?"

"Shit, you tell me."

"We can go in the bathroom, or out to my truck."

She took his hand and he followed her. She grabbed her keys off the table and walked towards the bathroom. Her thick body swayed from left to right. She had some meat on her bones just the way JC liked. "Let me potty first," she said as she went inside and left him by the door. He turned and looked over at Dee who was so into the game, he didn't care what was going on. Then he saw Akira, eyeing his bulge from his sweats pants. She tried to turn her head before he noticed.

Sara came out pretty quickly and grabbed JC's hand and they went out the door to her truck. She had a new all black Yukon truck with tinted windows. Right when they got up to the car door, she stopped him, and rushed him on the door and tongue kissed him aggressively as she was pulling his dick out of his sweatpants. Before he knew it, she had squatted and was sucking his dick and stroking it like she was super head, herself. "Damn," he said, as he held onto her head. He viewed the street, and there was a car coming down the street, but he didn't care, and neither did she.

"Big dick," she said as she spit on it, and kept sucking it. She soon stood up and opened the back seat door. "Go in first," she told him, as he slid in, and she came right behind him. She took her pants off then climbed to turn on the radio. She put on a song by Est gee & Jack Harlow, called The Department. She put it on repeat and started back sucking his dick as he enjoyed. The music was pretty loud, but he could still hear her making slurping noises.

She soon, got up and sat on his dick, and rode him, popping her booty up and down on his hard dick. "Shit! Shit!" she shouted as her tits bounced up and down in his face. JC slid under a little more to gain a better position, then he started fucking her hard and fast from the bottom. "Ah! Ah! Ah! Ah!" she hollered after each stroke he gave her.

"Turn over, let me see that ass," he said, as he smacked her ass cheek and it jiggled. It was so soft, and moved every time he touched it. She stretched out across the seat and tooted her ass up. JC jammed his dick inside her puddle and started deep stroking her hard and fast. All you heard was loud smacking noises and loud screams like she was getting raped. Good thing the radio was loud, that helped to smother some of the sound out.

JC had her ass cheeks spread as he was pounding her from the back repeatedly. "Ah! Ah! Ah! Daddy! Daddy! Ok Daddy!" she was screaming as he gripped her waist and continued.

"This the dick you wanted?"

"Yes! Daddy! Yes! Yes!"

He smacked her ass cheek hard as he slowed down a little and caught his breath. "I'm about to cum in this muthafucka."

"Yes! Daddy, cum in me!" she moaned as she still felt his dick slamming inside her. He picked his speed back up and she wished she had something to squeeze or even bite. JC was tearing her pussy up, and she was taking it all with plenty of loud screams. She felt him pushing her back down so she could arch and soon he was cumming.

"Arrrrgggghhh! Shit!" He came inside her and pulled his dick out once he was done. "You got something for I can wipe my dick off?"

She turned around and sucked all her juices off him, "That should do until we go inside."

They got out and went back in. Her hair was all over her head and she was walking a little wobbly. Akira just stared when they walked in and kept dancing. Dee was still on the game. JC went straight to the bathroom and Sara went to talk to Akira.

Chapter 58

"I can't believe you just fucked him in your truck like that. You was loud as hell."

Sara giggled. "Sorry."

"Well it was clearly good. I guess I don't have to ask that."

"So good. Like really good."

They both giggled.

"Fix me a drink," Sara told her and Akira got right on it. "Girl, you don't even know. He's daddy for sure."

Akira giggled and shook her head. "Such a slut."

"Girl he was so big," she whispered.

"Clearly. The way you was screaming. I almost came out there and hit the window. The neighbors was out there right on the porch. I know they heard everything."

"I don't care. I enjoyed myself."

They started giggling and JC soon came out the bathroom and sat down with Dee. "What up my nigga? You tryna get down?"

"Naw, I'ma watch you," JC said as he checked a text from Roxi.

Roxi: Goodnight baby. I have to be up early to leave for this drive. So have a good night. I'll text you in the morning.

JC: Goodnight boo. Talk to you tomorrow.

That night they all didn't go to sleep until about 3 in the morning. Sara stayed over and slept on the pull-out bed couch with JC. They fucked again and Sara was gone by 9 the next morning. When JC woke up he just sat up in the bed and was texting Roxi, then started swiping on Tinder. There were a lot of pretty girls on there and he kept swiping right. Although he loved his black women, there were so many foreign women, he wanted to see what they were about.

Akira came walking out the bedroom with some super tight shorts on that were light yellow see through. She went to the fridge and was bending over, where JC could really see her pussy print. "Good morning," she said, looking for whatever she was looking for.

"Good morning. Dee up?"

"No, he's still sleep. Want me to wake him up?"

"Naw, let him sleep. I was just asking."

"My friend Sara likes you."

"She do?"

"Yea, so don't be surprised if you see her over here a lot bugging you."

JC laughed, "She better take her ass to work or something and get her some money. I ain't about to be fucking her often like that and she ain't got no money."

She giggled, shocked. "You just going to let that big booty go to waste?"

"I don't care about that. She need some money to fuck with me. I gotta meet a girl with some money out here."

Chapter 59

"All the strippers got the money. And the girls that's selling they bodies. Sara not really like that."

"Shit she need to be selling it. It was good," he joked.

They both laughed. "You are so mean. I should tell her."

"Don't do that."

"Yea you might want to go to the strip club and get you one of them girls. But you have to be careful because these girls be having pimps out here."

"I'ma have to figure some shit out. You don't have any stripper friends?" he asked.

"Umm. I may know a couple girls."

"What's wrong?"

"Nothing, what?"

"I mean you like paused like you was unsure."

"It's Dee. He don't like me to have those kind of friends or whatever. He have accused me of doing stuff before just because the people I had in my circle." Her tone got lower.

"Ohhh I see."

"Yea. I mean its Vegas. Most of these girls you meet, especially if they cute, 8 times out of ten, have had sex with at least one celebrity here in Vegas. That's what I was being accused of."

JC laughed, "Oh damn, it's like that?"

"Yes. Sara knows. She's had her share."

"Of celebs?"

"Yes."

"Oh wow."

"Why you say wow?"

"That's just different. It's not like that where I'm from."

"Well, it's normal here, so get used to it."

"So, Sara be fucking celebs, but not getting paid?"

"I can't tell you all her business like that."

"You already started."

"I did, didn't I. Ok I'll say one last thing. Yes, she has some on speed dial. They give her a little money, but not like what she should be getting. She had one, that actually paid off her truck. I think she still deals with him when he comes in town. I'm not sure. Look, do not tell your cousin what I'm telling you about her. I love her, and she's my good friend. I know me and you don't know each other but I was just using her as a real-life example of what you may meet here in Vegas."

"Naw it's all good. I ain't about to say shit."

"I could tell you more stuff, but right now it's too soon," she said, walking away.

"Wait. What that mean?"

She did her fingers like she was saying bye bye, as she closed the room door. JC had a feeling she was into some shit that she wasn't saying, or maybe she knew some shit that could help him out that she wasn't saying. Either way, he wanted to know.

He swiped right on a chick, and it was a match. He viewed her pictures, and she was Latina, thick, nice body, nice lips, long black hair. Her name was Lily and after viewing her profile, he learned that she loved street tacos, and she liked to hike, watch movies, go to the gym and play tennis. He decided to message her.

Chapter 60

*J*C: How you doing? You looking good on your pics.

    Lily: That's all you got?

JC: What does that mean?

    Lily: Nevermind, hey.

JC: Damn was I supposed to come with some kind of introduction, or a pickup line or something?

    Lily: That's what most guys do on here. I enjoy reading them.

    JC: What you on this site looking for? I aint tryna waste your time or mine.

    Lily: I don't know, I'm just browsing really. It's too many assholes on here. So, I just be on here when I'm at work. Just for fun.

    JC: So, you haven't dated one person from on here?

Lily: Nope.

JC: Why not?

Lily: Dudes lame.

JC: Where you from?

Lily: Right here in Vegas.

JC: And you don't even like your own kind?

Lily: That's correct.

JC: So you Mexican?

Lily: Yes sir.

He was ready to block her, she clearly was on there for some other reason he couldn't guess. He went to his notifications and noticed some more matches. One was a black girl he had swiped. She had also sent him a message.

Vicky: It's about time a black man have swiped me.

JC: Damn it's like that?

Vicky: There's not many black men in Vegas that like black girls apparently.

JC: Oh shit.

Vicky: That's what I'm screaming over here. How are you?

JC: I'm good and you?

Vicky: Better now, now that I'm talking to you.

JC: Where you from?

Vicky: Texas but I've been up here for about 2 years. I love it. What about you?

JC: I'm from Michigan. I been here for a couple days.

Vicky: New new in Vegas. How you liking it so far? Welcome to Vegas.

JC: Thank you. I like it so far.

Vicky: Have you met anyone on here yet?

JC: Nope, you like the second person I've texted so far. I'm just trying to get familiar with the app.

Vicky: Well you mighty handsome, I hope I can keep your attention.

JC: We shall see. What you on here looking for? I see you looking good on your pictures. That booty real?

Vicky: Lmao yes, it's real! I'm just trying to date and meet someone cool. I've been on a couple dates off here, but no one I was interested in. Cool conversation but when we met in person, didn't really look like the pictures.

JC: That thang look nice. I don't believe it's real, I gotta see it in person. Oh, so you den got cat fished on here?

Chapter 61

*V*icky: *You so funny, you can see it. Pull up lol. Yes, a light version of catfish, because they were the same person, but looked messed up in person.*

JC: You will have to pull up on me. My car ain't here yet.

Vicky: Do you really have a car?

JC: Lmao! Yes, I have car.

Vicky: I'm just asking. Because I'm cool if you don't.

JC: I feel you. You must don't have a car and want me to be ok with you not having one.

Vicky: Lmaooooooo!!!!! I'm crying over here! No, I have a car. No worries. So let me know when you want me to pick you up.

JC sent his number to her and told her to call him, and she did within seconds. "Hello."

"Hiii!"

"Damn you sound sexy on the phone."

"Thank you. So, what you doing?" she asked.

"Nothing much just woke up for real. I drank a lil' bit too much last night."

"What you be drinking?"

"I prefer dark, like Henny or something. But last night they had me drinking vodka."

"I like tequila. I like to take shots."

"I can drink that too. When we linking and taking some shots?"

"I gotta make sure you not a serial killer first."

They both laughed.

"You ain't gotta worry about that. Even if I was a serial killer, I ain't got a reason to kill your little sexy butt."

She giggled.

"How tall are you?" he asked.

"I'm 5ft. 5" and you?"

"5ft. 11."

"So, are you here to stay or you just visiting?"

"I'm here to stay. I'm trying something new."

"How many baby mommas you got?"

JC laughed. "What the hell? You just going to assume I got a lot of baby mommas like that? That's probably why the black dudes ain't messing with your ass."

She giggled. "Shut up. Naw, the black guys out here, I swear do not be fucking with black women."

"Why not?"

"I'm not sure."

He laughed. "You know why."

"Why?"

"All these sexy ass foreign women out here. Niggas be wanting to try some new shit I'm sure. Then they find they self stuck."

"Mmh hmm."

"The guys you went out with was black or another race?"

"They were black. I'm not saying all the black guys like that, but most are that's here. You never answered my question when I asked you how many baby mommas you had."

"I don't have any. How many baby daddy's you got?"

"One. I have three little ones."

"Damn, you been getting it in."

She giggled. "I guess."

Chapter 62

He went to her profile to see how old she was. She was 27. "The father still in the life?"

"Yes, we have a good parenting relationship."

"He still be trying to hit that thang every now and then?"

"Naw, he actually don't."

"Oh, you be chasing him for dick then."

"No, I'm good on that."

"Let me get up and shower, eat and all that good stuff. I'ma lock your number in and hit you up later."

"Ok that's cool. Nice meeting you. Don't forget about me."

"I won't."

JC hung up and he had text messages and messages on Tinder from chicks. First, he checked his text messages, it was Roxi.

Roxi: Good morning handsome.

JC: Good morning gorgeous.

Roxi: Did you sleep good?

JC: I tossed and turned. What about you?

Roxi: I slept great, I'm not sore anymore lol. Why was you tossing and turning?

JC: Thinking about you and them pictures that you sent me. I wanted to call you but I knew you needed your rest.

Roxi: Oh my God JC, you could have called me. Anytime. I'm available anytime for you.

JC: Now I know. I wasn't sure.

Roxi: I'm going to need you to be extra sure. I'm here for you. I didn't even want to take this trip, because I wanted to be with you.

JC: When you come back, we have plenty of time. I'm glad your soreness is gone. I been missing that.

Roxi: I miss it too, I can't wait to have some more.

JC: You can have as much as you want when you get back.

Roxi: Can't wait.

JC went to the Tinder app and checked his messages. Lily had messaged back, and another chick had messaged.

Lily: What you doing today?

JC: Linking up with you to get some street tacos. I never had them.

Lily: What? You never had street tacos? You are missing out.

JC: I don't even know what they are.

Lily: I'm going to have to take you to my special place. The best in Vegas.

JC: I'm ready.

Lily: What part of Vegas you live in?

JC: Shit I don't know. I will have to ask, I just moved here like two days ago.

Lily: Ohhh ok ok. Well, are you closer to the new strip or the old strip?

JC: Lol I will have to ask once my cousin wakes up.

Lily: You just out here lost in the middle of nowhere huh?

JC: Yes, save me!

Lily: Lol, I'm about to put my cap on.

JC: Thank God.

Chapter 63

About a minute later, she was sending her phone number so JC could call her. He called right away.

"Hello."

"Hey, this JC from Tinder."

"Hi, how you doing?"

"Good and you?"

"I'm good. So, are you lying about you don't know what street tacos are?"

JC laughed. "Naw, I'm telling the truth. Where is the good ones?"

"We can meet there later if you want. I'll send you the address now."

"Ok that works. So, what's up with you? You sound different over the phone. You was a little dry in the messages," he said.

"It's so much trash on that site, so I don't know. I'm never taking it serious."

"I'm new on there, I can't relate yet, but you seem cool. You seem like a face to face person though."

"You are exactly right. We will talk more later on when we meet," she told him. She was so tired of wasting time conversating with guys.

"Ok that's cool, I'm going to lock your number in."

"Ok, cool beans."

He hung up and shook his head. She was a little weird to him but he was going to see what she was about anyway. JC got in the shower and got himself together. When he came out, Dee had came out the room. "What up, my nigga?"

"Shit, just showered right quick. I need to go get some clothes, just a couple pair of basketball shorts. That's all a nigga need out here. It's hot as fuck."

Dee laughed. "For sure, I'll have Akira take you up to the Nike store. I have to go handle some business."

"What you got going on nigga? I want in," JC said as he crossed his arms, grinning.

Dee smiled, "I told you, I be on the scamming shit. Just some credit card shit. I'm meeting up with a dude that's selling me some info on some shit."

"I need to get some of that shit and order me some clothes and shoes."

"Oh, that's easy. I'll get you some shit where you can order some shit online. It's going to be in like a week though."

"That's cool. I'ma grab some shit today and that will hold me over."

"Ok bet. You hit Sara last night?"

"Hell yeah, beat that thang down too, twice."

"Damn twice? I heard ya'll last night. Well, I heard her moaning and calling you daddy."

JC laughed. "Man, that bitch be too damn loud."

"She had some good good?"

"Hell yea, that pussy official for sure."

"See she the type that will let a nigga get her car and all that shit."

"Oh yeah?"

"Hell yea, my nigga used to be hitting her. She used to buy him shit, little shit though, but he used to take her to work and have her whip all day. So, I'm just giving you heads up on that. All you gotta do is ask her."

Chapter 64

"Good looking, shit I might need her truck tonight. I met this one chick on Tinder," JC showed him on his phone.

"Oh yeah, she nice," Dee confirmed.

"I'ma meet her at a taco place later on today probably."

"That's cool. What happened to the girl from the bus?"

"She in Cali right now. That's my lil' baby. I'ma make her my baby momma. I like her little sweet ass. You ain't try to mess with the friend, the Asian girl?"

"Yea we be texting and shit. She wanted me to come over and stay the night, but I can't stay no nights, my girl gone be tripping. So, I gotta find a way to hit her and leave."

"Tell her you work nights. Stop by her crib, right before you supposedly about to go to work. Hit her and you out."

"That's a good idea. I'ma use that."

"So, the strippers out here be giving nigga's money and shit?"

"I mean I guess so. It's a lot of pimps out here. I'm not really in that field, so I don't know how it works. All my niggas got girls and married or about to get married. Nigga you the pimp, I'm sure you will figure it out fast, you already fucked two badd chicks and you ain't even been here a week."

They both laughed.

"For real. I brought one of my homeboys from Atlanta here a couple months ago. He tried to hit Sara, and she ain't let him. He said she was tryna get him to buy her a purse or some shit. He was here for a whole week, and on the last night here, he ended up just using one of the escort services to fuck a chick."

"What he ugly or something? Fat?"

"Naw, he decent, got money, got his own business and shit."

"He try Tinder? It seems like the chicks on there on go."

"Yea he did Tinder. Akira set his page up, and he said he didn't have enough time to fuck a chick off Tinder."

"Oh naw, he was bullshitting. He probably wasn't aggressive enough on these hoes. That's what it sounds like."

"I don't know. But I do know that nigga had to pay $300 for some pussy. He fucked one chick the week he was here."

JC just shook his head.

"You going to the Mayweather fight this weekend?"

"Nigga it's going to be so many people in Vegas, even if you don't go to the fight, you going to think you were there by the time the weekend is up."

JC laughed. "Damn, that shit be lit like that?"

"Man, hell yea!"

"Should I get something to wear?"

"It don't matter. It's going to be plenty of bitches for everybody. You can go to the strip in some basket shorts, and a wife beater, the hoes going to be on you because of your body. See out here, you don't have to do much to attract pretty women. You just have to be in the right places. Most guys here, that really have money, you wouldn't be able to tell with what they wearing. They don't be having all that jewelry and stuff on. I mean don't get me wrong, you going to see shit like that, like when you pass a rapper or something. But the chicks, here, be on the dudes with the real money. I don't know how they find them, but they be having them."

Chapter 65

"**D**amn, that's crazy. You don't be hitting licks out here?" JC asked, as he had already tested Dee, by dropping a hundred dollar bill out his pocket. Dee had picked it up and never told him about it.

"Like robbing and shit? Sometimes, if the opportunity, presents itself, I'll do some shit. Why, what's up?"

"Shit I'm tryna get some money."

Dee leaned back and thought about it for a second. "I may have a few people in mind. At least we can see what's up. I got these Asian dudes that be growing weed. I've middle man some shit before multiple times. I can call them up, tell them we might be interested in like 25 pounds or something. The most I've got from them was 10, but that was like 6 times."

"They don't be having guns and shit when you come through?"

"Nope. I think It would be easy. And they be having all that shit on them."

"I mean I got two guns with me if they do," JC grabbed his bag and pulled them out. Dee looked around and made sure Akira wasn't around.

"Damn these some nice ass guns." Dee started looking at them and the name it had on it. "I got a 38 special in there too. I think we will be good with these."

"If it's that easy, I'm tryna get the most we can get. Tie them niggas up and make them tell us where all that shit at."

"I'm down. I got the number whenever you ready."

"After the fight weekend, we will see what's up."

"Bet, do you still want to go to the Nike store or something?"

"Yea."

Dee went in the room and asked Akira to take him to the store. 15 minutes later, she came out of the room with her keys in her hands. "You ready?"

"Yea."

They walked out the door and she had a small BMW, a few years older than the current year. JC tried to sit inside but the leather seats were super-hot. "Shit!" he said as he jumped when his butt hit the seat.

She giggled, "Oh yeah, you going to have to get used to this heat out here," she said, starting the car, and turning on the seat coolers. It only took seconds before he was able to sit down comfortably.

"What you about to get?"

"Some shorts and shit. Just something comfortable to wear. It's hot out here so I'm tryna be in the least clothes possible."

"Yes, sometimes it gets all the way up to 115 degrees."

"That's hot as hell."

"It's not like that where you from?"

"No. Not at all. It will get to like 100 or a little over, but then they calling heat advisory and all kind of shit."

She giggled. "Dang."

Chapter 66

"So why you go in the room on me earlier? I'm tryna get some money out here."

"I told you what you gotta do. You gotta get you a stripper. 99% of them sell pussy too so don't believe them if they say they don't."

JC laughed. "How you know?"

"These guys have money out here. If you was a girl, and a guy offered you, let's just say $5,000, for just one night. He don't live here, probably won't be back until next year. He just want to have a good time while he's here. You not going to do it?"

"Me personally? I'm doing it."

They both started laughing.

"I don't believe all girls would though." JC said.

"That was a low number. Ok, $20,000. You think she going to do it then?"

"Hell yea, she better."

"These are multimillionaires, that's nothing for them. I've heard about girls getting more money than that. But really, I think you should really be patient. You only been here a few days. Once you start mingling and going out, you will figure things out and get what you looking for."

"I feel like you got some stripper friends you can introduce me to."

"Why don't you just go to one of the strip clubs and see what you can find. We have plenty of them here."

"I guess I will try that. But I still think you hiding something from me. It's cool though. I'll give you a pass since you don't know me that well yet."

She giggled, "Oh I get a pass? Thanks. How sweet."

"Yea I'ma give you a pass. I can see you think I'ma tell on you, and get you dumped."

She giggled again, "That is not the case. Dee will never leave me," she said with confidence.

"Why is that?"

"Because he knows better."

JC laughed. "What the hell that mean?"

"Just know, he will never leave me."

"Ok that's starting to sound a little scary. I'ma leave that one alone."

They both laughed.

"Once I get to know you better and see how you move I'll see what I can do for you."

"Meaning?" he asked curious.

"I may be able to point you in the right direction. You never know."

174

"Why can't you just do that now?"

"I already told you. I don't know you. Or trust you like that."

"So, what do we need to do to establish some trust? I'm trying to make some money out here."

"Time."

JC smiled. "Akira, what you got going on? I'm not about to tell on you. I ain't trying to be in the middle of you and Dee shit. What you do or don't do ain't got nothing to do with me. I'm staying out of that one."

"Time, JC. Just be patient."

"It's hard to be patient when a nigga need money. How long I gotta wait?"

"Until you figure out what's going to make me trust you. If you gone have some dirt on me. I'ma need some on you as well."

"Ohhh, I see. I'm not in Vegas to have dirt on anyone and hold it over their head. I don't get down like that at all."

"I hear you."

"I'm serious."

"That's your cousin though."

"I ain't got no dirt about myself to give you, so I don't know what it's gone take."

"Well...You can give me some of what you gave Sara."

Chapter 67

JC turned and look at her and she was dead ass serious. "Damn. That's how you want to do this?"

"I mean, that way we have dirt on each other. You can't tell on me, and I can't tell on you. We will be locked in."

JC gave a small laugh, "And then what I get out the deal?"

"You get some good pussy, good head from me. Then I'ma going to put you with a chick I know, that's getting some real money. More money than most of the hoes you will meet in the strip club."

"How do I know you not just trying to play me?"

She pulled out her phone and started showing him some pictures of the girl she was talking about. The girl looked just like the Instagram model, Brittanya. She had her ass done, tits done, and she was a beautiful Mexican chick with tattoos. She had pictures, inside Rolls Royce's, Lamborghini's, Range Rovers, on beaches, inside beautiful mansions. "Damn, ok. So, she is who you going to introduce me to?"

"Yep."

"What if she don't fuck with me?"

"She will. She will do anything I ask her to do."

"Why don't you work with her and make that kind of money?"

"Because she does a lot. I'm just not ready for all that. She's 30 and been trying to get me to since I was 16. I know if I tell her you are family, and to help you, she would for sure. She knows all kind of people all over Vegas."

"So, if we have sex, then what? How long is it going to take you to connect me with her?"

"About two weeks. We not just having sex one time though."

JC laughed and shook his head and then she laughed as well. "You not getting no dick from Dee?"

"Yea, sometimes."

"So, what's the problem?"

"It's only when I initiate it." Even then, I still get turned down. Once a month if I'm lucky."

"So, when do this start? You going to have to keep your friend Sara away. I'm not about to be fucking her freely like that."

"We start asap. Whenever I want to do it though."

"Damn you asking for a lot."

"You are too. I don't even know you to be introducing you to someone like this. This girl have money. So you can crawl at the bottom in Vegas until you figure it out or you can go straight to the top. Do we have a deal or not?"

Chapter 68

JC sat there and thought about what she was saying. He was there to make some money and hopefully start a new life.

"Don't make me fuck you and Dee up out here in Vegas. You better be real smooth with this shit. We got a deal," he said and extended his hand when they were stopped at the red light.

"No, no, kiss," she said, leaning over and meeting him halfway for a kiss. Just a peck on the lips.

That kiss felt so weird to JC, and he felt like he just made a horrible deal, but he would make her regret it if she didn't come through on her end of the bargain. "You are crazy," he said, grinning.

"Whatever, relax. I got you," she told, him, as she winked at him. She turned her music up and started dancing sexy to some Spanish song that she played.

Once they made it to the Nike store, Akira just followed behind him as he tried on shoes, and picked out some shorts and t-shirts. She told him which ones were cute and which ones she didn't like. He took her advice and bought the ones she liked and they were out of there.

When they got back to the house, Dee was gone still so Akira called him to see where he was at.

"Hi baby, where are you?"

"Taking care of what I told you. What's up with you?"

"Nothing just got back. What are we going to eat?"

"I don't know. You have anything in mind?"

"Not really. I just know I'm hungry."

"See if JC hungry too. I'll just bring something if you want me too."

"He said he was, I just didn't want to do anything extra. I just came straight back."

"You want to go get something? Or ya'll want to wait until I get back?"

"I can wait. Let me ask JC." She asked JC and he didn't care. She then waved for JC to come in the room with her. She told him to be quiet.

"No, he said he will wait baby."

"Ok, cool. Hold on baby," Dee said as he clicked over.

Akira had started sucking JC's dick as he stood up on the side of the bed. She whispered, "It's so big." She was still holding the phone and sucking at the same time.

"You a dirty lil' slut," he whispered.

"Sure is," she said, still sucking and deep throating. Saliva was dripping on the floor as she was gagging.

"Mute that, you tripping."

"It's mute, relax, I got this," she said, still sucking. And soon Dee clicked back over.

"My bad, my bad. So, you think about what you wanted? Or have a taste for?" he asked.

"You feel like getting some spaghettis maybe from that Capone spot?" she said, as she was stroking JC dick with her hand while holding the phone with the other. JC was shaking his head and laughing in his head about how slick these chicks were. He made her get up as he pulled down her pants halfway and made her bend over the bed. She eased one leg out to put it on the bed.

"Shit that sounds good. You want the same thing you always get? Or you want what I be getting?" he asked then started talking in the background. "Come on Mark, you can do better than that. Last time I let you win. You gotta let me win sometimes too."

By the time she was able to respond, JC had his whole dick inside of her. He didn't want to move much though. He wasn't trying to alert him. She had some wet, tight pussy. Just being inside her sitting still, it felt good. It was soft inside her. She started bouncing her ass a little before she stopped and said, "Same thing I usually get." She then muted it, and JC started stroking her just a little, not too much.

"Ahh shiiit, it feels so good," she said as she reached back and pulled one of her ass cheeks apart, "Get all in there!" she moaned, "Shit!" she shouted, as he pressed harder inside her.

"What should I get, JC? You think he like spaghettis?"

"I think he would want what you get."

"Ask him. No need to guess."

JC pulled out of her and ran to the living room and Akira, yelled, "JC, you like spaghettis?"

"Yea, that's cool. Make sure you get some garlic bread with it too."

"He said yes he likes spaghettis with garlic bread," she said and he was right back inside her, this time slipping right in as she was still bent over.

Dee laughed, "Ok bet. Anything else you need?"

"Nope."

"Ok, I got you. See you in a little bit."

"Ok."

Chapter 69

She hung up and tossed her phone across the room as JC started pounding her pussy like he was a mad man. "Ohh shit! Baby! Fuck!" she shouted as she took his dick but was trying to crawl away but he had her hips, pulling her back to him.

"Shit I'm about to cum!" he told her, as he kept stroking. Her ass was clapping up against his body as it made a loud smacking noise each time.

"No! Don't stop! I'm... going!" she screamed as she threw her ass back on his dick, taking all of him, "To...cum all over this dick!" she moaned.

"Fuck!" he growled and moaned.

"Please don't stop!" she shouted as he slammed into her over and over, going so fast he was starting to get dizzy.

"I can't hold it!" he said as he felt himself cumming inside her.

"Don't fucking stop!" she shouted as he slowed down but didn't stop and soon her body was shaking, as she orgasmed right after him. "Fuckkkk! I'm cumming all over this dick, oh my fucking God!" she screamed out as she clasped onto the bed trying to catch her breath.

JC was still inside her as he fell on top of her. Her pussy was like a pool of water. He felt his cum, her cum, and more wetness. He still stroked slow, trying to get all his out, plus letting her get her full sensation.

"That was...so good," she said, as she laid flat on the bed, with a sweat shiny face.

"I'm about to pull out," he said as he kissed the side of her face.

"Wait! Don't yet. It feel so good. One second," she told him. "Kiss me," she said, turning her face to the side to meet his lips. He tongue kissed her deeply, and finally he eased his dick out of her and watched her pussy lips drip cum between them. He smacked her ass hard. "Ow!" she shouted as she jumped and started smiling.

JC pulled up his pants and walked out and went to the shower. He knew he was playing with fire, but he had to do what he had to do. Akira had convinced him that she had the keys to what he was looking for. After he got out of the shower, Akira went right after. She came running out of the room and he smacked her on the ass as she walked past him. She couldn't stop smiling.

"Hey, you got an old iPhone that you don't use anymore?"

"I do, it's just a little old. But you can have it. I'll grab it for you real quick." She went and got it for him. "What you going to do with it? I have naked pictures in this phone. You better keep it safe."

JC laughed. "I will, I'ma just get it activated. I'm about to change my number."

"Ok. And don't tell Dee where you got this phone."

"He not going to even ask me no shit like that."

"Oh, good," she said as she closed the door and got in the shower.

Chapter 70

As JC went to go sit on the couch, Roxi was calling. "Hello."

"Hi baby. What are you doing?" she asked, sounding bubbly.

"Laying on the couch, thinking about you. Missing you. Can't wait until you come back."

"Aww, you got me blushing while I'm walking down this busy street. I so miss you too. Oh my God. So much."

"Why you walking down the street?"

"I'm at the fashion district. This what you basically do. There's all these stores on these different blocks and you go from store to store, buying different fabrics and stuff. It's so fun, you have to come one day with me. It will be fun. I can teach you some things."

"One day for sure. I'm down. That sound cool."

"You have any plans for the weekend? It's the big fight."

"Not really. I probably go to the strip with the fam but nothing much, hopefully you be back by then."

"Yes, I will for sure. You better make time for me. I really want to see you. I would ask you to Facetime, but I remember you already told me that you don't like pictures or Facetime."

"I'm glad you listening to me."

"Yes. I hear everything you say."

"Who you with out there?"

"Just some friends. We all do similar things, make clothes. None of my roommates though. But it's all girls and we are finding so much good stuff. That talk you had with me, have me so much more motivated. This is the most excitement I've had since when I first had the idea of doing this."

"Aww that's good baby," he said. He heard Akira running bath water after she took a shower. "Natali didn't go with you?"

"No, she had to work. I just got off the phone with her. Dee is going over there tonight. I think he's going to get some."

JC laughed. "That's cool. I'm sure he will tell me a little later on."

"Yea, she's so excited to see him. I'm like, I wish I was there, then you coulda came with him."

"Fasho."

"Ok, well I just wanted to call you and hear your voice. Let me know if I'm being annoying, ok? I'm a very like happy person, but I know, sometimes it can annoy people."

"You good baby. You not annoying me at all."

"Ok, great."

"Hit me up later on. Enjoy yourself and focus baby. Get something good. I might want you to model in it for me."

"Might? I most definitely wouldn't mind that!"

"Oh, I thought you was going to be acting shy about it."

"You're right," she giggled, "But for some reason, I feel comfortable with you. Well, you make me feel comfortable."

"How I do that?"

"Like when you tell me how beautiful I am. How good I look and all that sweet stuff you say to me when we are having sex," she said as her voice lowered.

"I be meaning every word."

"I know. I can just feel it all over my body when you say it to me."

"Aww."

She giggled, "I know. I think that's so sweet. I can't wait to see you again, JC. I'll talk to you later. Have an awesome day."

"Ok baby, you too."

Chapter 71

He hung up and was sitting there thinking for a minute. Vegas was a whole hand full already and he was loving it. He thought about meeting Lily later on so he texted Sara to see what she was going to be doing.

JC: What's up lil' buss it baby?

Sara: Lol, Hi!

JC: What you doing?

Sara: Helping my mom out, she wanted to purge today.

JC: Purge?

Sara: Lol clean the house, throw some things out.

JC: Oh, lol I didn't know that meant that. I thought about the movie instantly.

Sara: Haha cute.

JC: You coming to see me tonight?

Sara: For sure.

JC: What time?

Sara: You tell me and I won't be a minute late.

JC: Lol ok 7 and if you a minute late, I'ma cum all over your face.

Sara: I'ma be late on purpose now.

JC: Lmao smh. Ok nevermind. Be here, I need to use your truck to go somewhere when you get here.

Sara: Ok no problem. See you later.

JC laid on the couch until Dee came back with the food. They ate, and Dee was playing the game. He had told JC he was going to sneak over to Natali's crib later. JC thought it was a good plan and told him what he had planned with Sara and Lily.

Later that day, Sara came over and her and Akira started drinking. JC left around 8 o'clock to meet Lily and Dee left right after him to head over to Natali's. JC used the gps to get around. Even driving in Vegas, the vibe felt different to him. He didn't have a worry in the world. Vegas was the place to be in his eyes. There were so many bad chicks and he instantly felt like he had been cheated out of a better life. He started wishing he was born and raised in a place like this. Every time he used to hear about Las Vegas, he automatically thought about a party city, but it was way more than that. People really lived here and had lives.

Chapter 72

As he drove down the strip alone, the lights were amazing to him. Everything was lit up. Even the buses in front of him were lit up. People were walking, taking pictures, and having a great time. Traffic wasn't that crazy, but it was busy. Soon, he was pulling up to the place Lily had sent him. There were a lot of people lined up and a casino was right behind them. He didn't see a restaurant though, so he called her.

"Hello. Are you here?"

"Yea, but this don't look like a restaurant."

She giggled. "Nooo it's not a restaurant. It's a taco truck. Are you in this truck?"

JC laughed, "Oh. Yea, is that you waving?"

"Yes, come here and park."

He drove over and parked. As he was parking, he saw her, and she had a body like crazy. He knew her ass was fake for sure. He didn't even have to ask. He stepped out and she smiled.

"Hiii!" she said, as she opened her arms.

"Hey!" he hugged her and started checking her out. "Damn girl, you thicky thick." Her waist was small, ass fat and thighs big. She looked like a girl out of a magazine. She had heard that a lot, so she knew what he meant.

"This what you call, done up," she said as she twirled around for him.

"You sexy as hell."

"Thank you. You not too bad yourself."

"Thank you. So, this the taco spot? For some reason I knew not to try to even get dressed. I had a feeling."

"You're good with what you have on. It's just a taco truck."

"Ok cool. You going to have to order for me. I don't know what this shit is."

"You never ate Mexican food?"

"Nope, I don't think so."

"Oh my, ok, do you like steak or chicken more?"

"Steak."

"Ok, come on."

He followed her up to the long line. He couldn't believe how many people were standing in line waiting on this truck. He walked behind her and admired her body. He loved big booties, but she was overdoing it. Everyone was staring and even saluting him when he caught them looking.

It took over an hour just to order the food which she ordered in Spanish. They talked the whole time and JC could sense she was a gold digger. She was looking for a man with money. She was still cool and they ended up in her Benz, eating tacos and laughing together. They got along good.

"Yea these tacos is fire! What do I ask for when I want to order these again? You was up there talking Spanish and shit."

"What I tell you?" she said smiling from ear to ear. "They are the best. So you would order, carne asada, with cheese, onions and cilantro. Any Mexican girl you meet here, if you take her to this place she's going to fall in love with you."

JC laughed and took another bite of the small taco and soon his phone was ringing but he didn't answer. It was Sara. Then a text came through that he didn't open neither. Another number was calling next which he ignored.

"Damn, your phone blowing up like crazy."

"Ain't nobody important," he said looking at the time. It was a little past 10 o'clock. His phone kept ringing back to back until he answered a number he never even saw before. "Hello."

"JC, Dee is in the hospital. He just got beat up really bad. We on our way up there right now. Can you meet us there?"

Chapter 73

JC just listened and wondered what was going on. "Ok send me the address. I'll be on my way right now," he said as he dropped his taco on the aluminum foil.

"What happened? Is everything ok?"

"My cousin just got beat up real bad. He in the hospital."

"Oh my, go see about that. I hope he's ok."

"Yea. Let me go up here and see what's going on. I'll call you later."

"Ok. It was nice meeting you. Thanks for the tacos!"

"You welcome. Nice meeting you as well."

He got out, went to the truck, and headed to the hospital. Roxi had called crying, apologizing to him and telling him that she had heard what happened. JC told her to relax, that it was ok, and he would call her later. He called Akira phone back once he pulled up and her and Sara came out and got him. He walked in Dee's room, and they had him all hooked up to some IV's. He was swollen in the face, and his jaw was knocked off track, not broken, plus he had a concussion. He was awake though when JC walked in looking at him like what happened. Dee couldn't talk though but he reached for his phone and JC gave it to him.

Dee: Larry

JC: Wow, I'm fucking him up. You want me to wait until you get well or do it now?

Dee: Wait for me.

JC: Did you get some pussy?

Dee: Lol yea, he caught me leaving. Ran out of nowhere. I think it was two of them, I don't remember.

JC: Yea he gone pay for that. Don't even worry about that one.

Dee: Fasho.

An hour had went by fast and Sara was trying to get JC outside to the truck but he turned her down. She waited around for a little more time then left. By the time it was 1am he was about to get some surgery and they were keeping him overnight. JC and Akira headed home, and she was sad.

"Why would they do that to him?"

"Shit happens. He will be alright."

"Did he tell you who did that to him?" she asked.

"Naw."

"Are you hungry?"

"Not really. You?"

"No. I was just making sure you wasn't, I remember you was saying you was eating some tacos and had to stop eating."

"Oh, naw I'm good."

Chapter 74

They finally made it home, and JC got his bed ready, pulling it out of the couch and laying down. Akira came out of the room wearing some red boy shorts and a small t-shirt. Her ass was jiggling as she walked and locked all the doors. She locked the top lock where no one could get in even with a key. This lock was only for the inside. "You going to sleep?" she asked.

"In a second. What's up?"

She didn't say anything. She just walked over to him and climbed on top of him and pulled his dick out and started sucking it. "Ok," he said as he laid back and enjoyed. His dick raised straight up and she started taking off her boy shorts and her shirt.

"Take all that off," she told him. He got butt naked with her, showing his muscular body. It turned her on even more as she laid him down, climbed on top of him and sat on his dick slowly. "Mmmm," she moaned as she slid all the way down. She then began riding him slowly. "How does this pussy feel to you?" she asked as she worked her hips.

"This pussy feels good, baby," he responded while looking her in her eyes. He was mind blown by all these beautiful women he kept connecting with and having sex with. Akira was looking so sexy to him while she was riding his dick. He could tell his dick was more than enough for her by the look of her facial expressions. She was moving so slow and being extra careful.

"I'm so happy you inside me. I was so sad, but this dick make me so happy," she moaned, still working his dick inside her. "Is my pussy wet enough?"

"It's so wet and soft."

"I'm going to cum all over this dick."

He responded by grabbing onto her hips and pressing up against her clit.

"Yes baby, just like that. I'm going to cum baby," she moaned as she closed her eyes and cringed.

"Cum on that dick baby. Cum all over that dick," he whispered, and she started shaking while still riding him. She dug her nails in his chest and made a loud screaming noise as she came hard. "Good girl," he whispered, and she kissed him for about 15 seconds before she sat back up. "Taste that cum. Clean that dick up."

"You want me to taste it, baby?" she asked in a sexy tone, while climbing off of him and sliding down, putting his dick into her mouth. She started licking all around his dick, licking her cum from all around it.

"What it taste like, beautiful?"

She climbed up and kissed him deeply, "What you think?"

"It taste good baby. Give me some more," he said, and she kissed him again while he slid his dick back inside her. "Damn you, some dangerous pussy. This muthafucka feel good as hell."

"You like it?" she asked, still kissing him.

"Yes," he said as he worked his hips, going in circles in her pussy as she straddled him.

"Ohh baby!" she moaned as she continued to kiss him.

"That feel good?"

"Yes baby," she moaned and put her head on the side of his neck. He gripped her ass cheeks and started fucking her while she just laid on him, moaning in his ear. "Oh my God baby," she whispered as she felt him going all kinds of places inside her. "Baby," she moaned.

"Talk to me baby," he said, stroking away.

"You gonna me make me cum so good, don't stop," she moaned. JC continued to fuck her like he was making love to her pussy. She was so wet, and her walls were squeezing on his dick so perfectly. "Baby," she moaned as she put both her hands on each side of his neck tightly.

"Yes, beautiful?" he whispered.

"I'm cumming baby," she said, squealing as she tensed up and let out a big scream. JC kept going slowly and she was kissing him again and seconds later he was cumming inside of her.

"Damn baby," he whispered, as he gripped her ass, shooting cum inside her. "This pussy fire, God damn."

He stopped moving, and she laid on top of him, kissing his face. "Please don't stop fucking me even when I introduce you to my friend."

JC laughed. "That wasn't part of our deal though."

"I know," she whined. "But I didn't know it was this good. Can I renegotiate please?" she asked, kissing him on the lips.

"I'ma think about it."

"Ok."

She fell to sleep with his dick still inside her. By the next morning, they were lying beside each other as the bright sun, woke them both up. Akira got up, went and got in the shower, checked her phone, but Dee hadn't called. She got dressed and was about to head up there. "JC, I'll be back. Call me if you need anything," she said, kissing him on the cheek.

He was still laying there, going through his phone. Roxi had texted numerous times. Lily had texted, sending him a pussy picture. He texted her back.

Chapter 75

*J*C: *That pussy looking nice.*

   Lily: You want some?

JC: *Sure.*

   Lily: *You need to know the price tag? Or you the type of guy that don't ever have to look at price tags?*

   JC: *How much?*

   Lily: *How long?*

   JC: *All night.*

   Lily: *$2,500.*

   JC: *Lol*

   Lily: *?*

   JC: *You tripping.*

   Lily: *You blocked.*

   JC: *Fuck you.*

   Lily: *Fuck you, broke ass nigga.*

   JC cracked up as he tried to send her another message but she had blocked him. He shook his head knowing it was something with her. She was on there trying to make her money. He couldn't be mad at that. He was shocked at how much she charged though.

JC: Good morning, yes he is ok. Been up there all night.

Roxi: I'm so sorry. I'll be back tomorrow. Please forgive me for that. Now you see why I haven't had a boyfriend in so long. Because I couldn't. I hope this don't run you away.

JC: Don't worry about that. I'll take care of it. It's ok. I'm not going anywhere.

Roxi: Ok. I cried for so long last night. I didn't know what to do or what I should do.

JC: Relax, it's not your fault at all.

Roxi: I'll tell you whatever you want to know about him. I told you his full name already. I'm so sorry what happen to your cousin.

JC: Baby it's ok.

Roxi: I miss you so much.

JC: I miss you too. I'm going to text you later. I'm about to go see how my cousin doing.

Roxi: Ok baby, have a great day.

JC: Thank you, you too.

Chapter 76

JC had dozed back off to sleep and woke up when he heard the door open. It was Akira and Dee, "They let you out of there?" JC asked as he stretched.

"Yea, I'm straight. I thought my jaw was broken, but it was just knocked out of place. I just gotta rest the next few days that's all."

"That's cool. Glad to see you good."

"I didn't get any food. Not sure if you hungry or not, JC," Akira said, taking off her purse. She was wearing some white short shorts, where her ass cheeks was hanging out of the bottom. JC couldn't help but get a glance every now and then. Dee had went straight to the room and put on the game.

"Where's some good breakfast?"

"I know of a good place that's not too far from here. You like pancakes?"

"Yea, with eggs and bacon please. Orange juice for the drink."

"Ok," she said before going in the room to assist Dee then leaving to go get the breakfast. JC went in the room with Dee.

"You good nigga?"

"Yea, I'm good. I'm just about to heal up then we can go take care of that."

"Fasho, Roxi been giving me all the info to where that nigga at. We can go get him whenever. What you tryna do to him? Obviously that nigga can take an ass whopping."

"What you was thinking about? Killing him?"

"I mean, that's up to you," JC said, not wanting to come right out with his real answer. He noticed Dee's fake smile when he asked.

"Naw, I ain't tryna kill him. I ain't tryna go to jail or nothing."

"I mean it's ways to do shit without going to jail. But I feel you. So, what you just want to get your lick back?" JC said with a slight laugh.

"Yea, nothing crazy."

"Shit karma get niggas like that all the time, so you never know what may happen to him before we get to him."

"Yea karma is a bitch for sure."

JC had plans on killing him, he wasn't about to keep playing the fighting game. He had to kill him, because he didn't see Larry stopping. Or maybe he could cripple him. Either way, he wasn't trying to keep fighting him like Dee wanted to do. JC knew what would work. "So how was the pussy?"

Dee smiled, "Man, she's a freak. I fucked the shit out her ass. Had her screaming my name and everything. She been texting me all morning. I almost got caught, because Akira came early this morning, and I had fell back to sleep with my phone right on the side of me. It was text messages all down my phone when I woke up."

"Aw man, that wouldn't have been good."

"Hell naw it wouldn't. Oh, I looked your guns up on the internet. Man, you can get $4,000 for each one of those. The place that buys them right in Vegas too."

"Shit I'll sell one for sure right now."

"I'll have Akira take you later on. They will cash you right out for it. I think they sell them for like $6,000-$7,000, but they pay $4,000 for them."

"That's cool with me. I need that shit right now."

"That will hold you over until I heal up. Then we can go do some shit."

"Damn you ain't even going to be able to hit the fight with me."

"Hell naw, Akira already planning to order it, and have people over here so I'll be chilling."

"That's cool. I'ma go with Roxi to the strip then, and spend some time with her."

"Yea, you going to see a lot of badd bitches."

JC laughed. "Man I already been seeing a lot. When me and Akira went to that Nike store, it was so many badd bitches in there, I'm like what the fuck."

They both laughed.

Chapter 77

 ""Last night, I met up with this lil' badd Mexican chick with a fat ass booty. It was too big though, but we met at a taco truck. The line was so damn long."

"I know exactly where you talking about too, fire."

"Hell yeah. We was standing there talking and shit. We had a good lil' date. We was sitting in her Benz and shit. She was tryna feed a nigga and shit. This morning, she sent me a pic of the pussy. I'm thinking she tryna fuck, this bitch turned around and said $2,500 to fuck. I'm like, bitch, you tripping."

They both laughed.

"Yea nigga, them bitches that be looking like they got work done and shit, be taxing. They got that work done just to make money. I den been set up a few times too. I had this Korean and Italian bitch I had met on this other app, called Plenty of Fish. Bitch badd as hell. She tell me to meet her at the mall, so I did. This after about of week of phone and text messages. So, I meet her at the mall, the fancy mall too. She was in this high-end designer store trying on shit. She letting me come in the dressing room with her, showing me her ass, letting me feel on her and everything right. She was twerking on me and all," he said, laughing. "We walk up to the cash register, so I fall back a little and let her take care of her business, you know. She got three pieces she about to buy. So I'm chilling just waiting. She calls me over there and shit, so I walked up and she's pointing at the total, looking at me. I'm like, what?" He laughed again. "The total like $1,873 or something. I'm like, I ain't bring no money, baby."

They bust out laughing.

"Especially that kind of money, bitch!" JC added.

"Right! So, she look at me like I was crazy. It's people behind us and everything. She tells the cash register lady to hold her items for a second and take care of the other people. Man, listen, that shit was so embarrassing. The girl on the register was badd too, and was looking at me like, really?" He started laughing again because JC kept cracking up. "So, look, the bitch pull me outside crying nigga, talking about this her favorite store and I embarrassed her. Why wouldn't I bring any money. All this stupid ass shit. Nigga, I just walked off."

JC was on the floor holding his stomach. "Dawg! You funny as fuck! Why she thought you had money?"

Dee laughed. "I told her I owned a couple bars on the strip."

JC laughed even harder.

"It works sometimes," Dee said, laughing as well.

JC and Dee talked for a while and soon Akira had come back with the food.

On fight night, they had company. Dee invited a few of his friends, and they all brought their girlfriends. JC left and went to the strip with Roxi. They walked around through the crowd down the whole strip that night. JC had a ball.

There was so much to see. Roxi was looking like a model. She was all dressed up, light make up, and her skin was glowing. JC was happy to be with her. She made him happy. He could just look at her and be happy. She had beautiful skin, beautiful lips, a beautiful body that was natural, and she was in great shape. He knew for sure, she was going to be his baby momma. There wasn't a doubt in his mind. Everything went great and they ended the Saturday night in Roxi's bed. JC had gotten drunk since all the drinks were pretty much free in every casino, they had went in. He flipped and fucked Roxi every which way he could think of. Since the house was empty Roxi was loud as she was moaning his name nonstop until they both were knocked out asleep.

They didn't get out of the bed until noon the next day. They laid up and had more sex. Neither one of them could get enough of each other. "I had so much fun last night."

"Me too," JC said as he changed the channel. Roxi was glued to him and was kissing him under his chin, and rubbing his chest.

"I love being around you, going places with you, having sex with you, cuddling with you. I just feel so safe with you."

He looked down and kissed her lips. "The feeling is mutual baby."

Chapter 78

They got out the bed around 2 o'clock. The sun was blazing outside when Roxi rolled over in bed and kissed JC awake. They lay there kissing lazily for a while before she told him that she needed to leave out. After grabbing a quick bite and shower, they went to a mall that was near her house. She had to grab a few things that she needed. JC needed a few things too. He had enough clothes for now but he needed some other things. He was going to grab a couple snap back hats. As soon as they arrived at the mall, JC did a triple take when he saw who was in front of him. He could barely believe his eyes.

"What?" Roxi asked, as she looked at him, and he looked like he had seen a ghost. His eyes were wide and his jaw had dropped as he stared at something. She couldn't figure out what it was that had him so spooked.

"Nothing," he said, smiling at her. He quickly shook himself and adjusted his expression. He secretly pinched his leg through the pocket of his shorts to make sure he wasn't dreaming. It couldn't be real but he seemed to be wide awake. This wasn't a dream.

"You sure?" she asked as she cruised around looking for a parking spot. JC was quiet and she didn't push him because she was busy trying to find a parking spot.

JC's heart started to pick up it's speed, thumping hard, loud and fast inside his chest that he was sure it was going to explode. He couldn't believe who he had just saw. Kelly and another white girl were walking up the parking lot as they were parking in the spot. He thought his eyes had betrayed him and he had mistaken some other girl for Kelly but once he had gotten a good look, he knew it was her. He swallowed hard and got out of the car as fast as he could, slamming the door behind him. He didn't want to lose sight of her. He knew she probably was in Vegas for the fight and hadn't left yet. It was just weird how he had managed to bump into her in such a big place.

"Turn the car off baby," he told Roxi as he noticed her get out as well and the car was still on. His eyes were still glued to Kelly, and he wasn't paying much attention to anything else at the moment.

She giggled and shook her head. "Baby it's going to be a hundred today. We leave our cars running sometimes when it's this hot."

"Oh damn. I didn't know that." he said, turning his attention back to Roxi, and they both laughed. As they were walking towards the mall through the packed parking lot, he noticed plenty of cars running with no one inside. "Damn they just leave the car running while they inside the mall and nobody in them," JC exclaimed with amazement.

Chapter 79

"Y es." She gave him a questioning look. "Why wouldn't they?"

"That couldn't happen where I'm from. They would come back out and not have a car."

They both laughed together as they walked.

"I'll hate to live there. Is it hot like here?" she asked, genuinely interested in learning more.

"Naw. Hell naw," he said, paying attention to where Kelly was as she was walking up ahead of him. She still had that nice body on her and still looked the same. She hadn't changed a bit since he had last seen her and now that he had run across her, he needed to figure out how to avoid her. He needed a plan. Roxi started holding his hand as they walked together, guiding him along as she talked to him animatedly, pointing at things in the stores they passed by. Every time he saw Kelly stop at a store, to avoid walking by her, he stopped at a different store a few dozen feet away and acted as if he wanted to check something out. He would act like he was interested in something, and Roxi fell for it every single time. She had no clue what he was up to. She really got into it, stopping and admiring what he was looking at. While she was distracted at the storefront, JC kept flashing glances at Kelly. He watched Kelly from a distance, as she shopped and bought small things. Roxi had made it to the store she had came for, and JC stepped inside, glad to finally make it out of Kelly's line of view. He turned his attention back to Roxi and made her try on different things as he let Kelly get way ahead of them. He stalled for as long as he could. He kept looking and spotting her each time. It seemed like she just wouldn't disappear from his sight.

"Baby," Roxi called as she came out, wearing a outfit she tried on for him. "Who you looking for?" she asked when she saw him looking out of the window. He turned back to her and shook his head, smiling at her.

"I thought I seen Dee," he said, brushing off her question. He looked at the outfit she was wearing and nodded. "I like that one. Spin for me," he said, smiling. She modeled for him and then disappeared back into the dressing room to try on the next outfit.

Chapter 80

While she was busy changing, which he knew would take a while, JC went out of the store because he had lost Kelly for a second then he saw her coming back that way. He went back in the store and Roxi now had on a new outfit. "I like that one too. I want to see the other one though," he said, rushing her back in the dressing room and closing the door. "I think this one will look better than all of them," he said.

She smiled, "Ok, I'll put this one on for you." She was being affectionate now that she felt that JC was giving her a lot of attention and compliments. She hugged and started kissing on him while he rubbed on her soft booty. He loved that she was so curvy in all the right places and a minute later, he broke away.

"Ok, you try that on and I'm going to run to a couple stores. Stay here until I get back," he told her, already halfway out of the store door.

"Oh," she agreed, going back into the dressing room to try on the other outfits JC had selected for her.

He left out and saw that Kelly stopped at a booth in the middle of the mall. He walked right past her and went out the door to the parking lot. People were all over the place coming and going out. The whole place was so busy that nobody spared another person a second look. Everyone was going about their own business, and this presented him with the perfect opportunity for what he had in mind since they had first come into the mall. JC searched the parking a lot for a car that was running. He was careful to stroll by like he was searching for his own car, and nobody seemed to care. He found a older model car that was running, so he walked up on it thinking he would have to break the window but surprisingly it was unlocked. Shaking his head at how careless people seemed to be in Vegas, he quickly pulled the door open. He hopped right in and backed up. He went up the aisle and went around and soon he was seeing Kelly and another girl walking out of the mall. Kelly stopped and put on her shades and swung her hair over her shoulder. They then walked up the aisle to the left and JC came up behind them. He thought about jumping out of the car right then and there and choking her out or even beating her up on the spot. He stopped to watch her and let them get ahead of him just enough. He then floored the car and ran right into her, her body hitting the bumper hard as it made contact. She flipped up over the car, her body flopping around like a ragdoll, and landed on her stomach, hitting her face on the steaming hot asphalt.

"Shit," JC said, not feeling like he got her good enough. He wished he had backed up a little more and got some momentum going, so he could have gotten her a lot better. He looked in the rearview mirror and saw her lifting up, with blood on her, coming from somewhere on her face. He quickly put the car in reverse.

He backed up and sped towards her. As the tires hit her, they rolled over her lower body this time. He felt each bump as he rode over both her legs. He could hear her screaming for help as he sped off once he saw all the people running towards the scene. He drove just a few blocks over and hopped out the car, leaving it abandoned by the side of the road, and started walking through some back yards, then up the street. He pulled out his phone and called Roxi up.

Chapter 81

"Where are you? You got me sitting in this dressing room and you wandering all over the mall," she whined.

"Can you pick me up? I'm at the gas station around the corner."

"Why you leave?" She sounded surprised since he'd told her he was just going to go look at some other stores.

"I got in the car with my cousin, then someone got ran over outside the mall so we came over here to the gas station. Come get me baby."

"Oh... Ok, I'm coming baby," she said. To his relief, he could hear her grabbing her bag and starting to walk out of the dressing room. "Do you want me to pay for this stuff or just come get you right now?"

"Come get me right now," he said as calm as he could. He was completely thrown by what had gone down and he needed to calm himself down before Roxi reached him, or otherwise it was all going to look very suspicious.

She drove over to where he was standing in less than a few minutes and JC jumped in and leaned his seat back a little as they drove away. "It's still a lot of people in the parking lot?" he asked, trying to sound casual.

214

"Yes. Police is everywhere. It's crazy over there. I was barely able to get to my car. I was just sitting there waiting for you in the dressing room like, where's my baby?" she giggled, reaching over to squeeze his upper arm. "I had start trying on other outfits. I took pictures for you and everything."

"My bad."

They drove back to her place. The minute they were inside the house, JC went straight to the tv, turning on the news station. He needed to know what was going on. He had been in the dark about the entire situation on the whole drive back and it had been driving him nuts. They didn't have a suspect according to the news and he breathed a sigh of relief. So far so good. JC was trying to see if Kelly was dead but she wasn't, much to his disappointment. She was just injured badly but still alive. He hit her pretty good, but not good enough. But he knew he had broke some bones at the very least. They rushed her to the nearest hospital.

"That's so messed up. What an asshole. Just to run someone over like that, is a heartless person. What is wrong with people in today's world?" Roxi said as she watched the news with him.

"Yea that's some messed up shit," JC said, shaking his head.

"That's so sad. I'm so glad you're safe." She hugged him and kissed him.

Chapter 82

Later that day, they went to another mall and finally got what they both had wanted. She got a few outfits, and he just grabbed some hats. On the way home, they drove past the hospital that was mentioned on the news. "Aww, we should stop and give her some flowers. That's the hospital where the girl at that got hit at the mall," Roxi said, slowing down as she glanced out of the window at the hospital.

"Aww, you too much of a sweetheart, keep it moving. Not today boo," JC said firmly.

JC thought about going up there but he knew the police would be all over whatever floor she was on. They stopped and got food and went back to Roxi's place.

He stayed inside with Roxi and barely went out, trying to wait until everything calmed down. The police were investigating and still didn't have a suspect. They did have a drawing, which looked nothing like JC. Kelly was in a coma and JC wanted to go up to the hospital and finish her off but he knew, Merido and whoever else was in town. Roxi's roommate worked at the same hospital and was giving JC info on Kelly. She had told him there were mob guys all through the hospital and they had already left a few people dead, due to the incident.

A couple days later it was night time when JC linked up with Dee, and they both sat on the street of where Larry lived at. They had parked on the side of the road. The street wasn't busy at all and the street lights no longer worked so darkness filled the whole area. JC was holding his gun, making sure his clip was full. "We don't need that. Why you even bring that?" Dee asked, curious. He didn't want to shoot Larry or kill him. He just wanted to beat him up and get his revenge back.

"What if he got a gun?"

"He not going to have a gun. Niggas in Vegas don't just be having guns on them like that unless they in a gang or something. Well at least not the niggas I've been around."

"I'ma just pistol whip the nigga."

"I say we don't even bring it at all," Dee said. For some reason, he didn't trust what JC was saying.

"Well, you got a hammer or something? I ain't about to play with that big ass nigga when I get in there."

"Yea I have one in the trunk." Dee hit the button and jumped out and grabbed the hammer from the trunk and gave it to JC.

"Yea, this will work," JC said as he shook his head up and down.

They waited there for a couple hours, and no one showed up. They both were texting while just chilling there in silence. JC was texting Roxi and Dee was texting Akira.

"You think we should hide up there on his porch or something?"

"Yea. Let's go," Dee said. They walked up to his house and first walked around it. It was empty. It was dark inside, but a tv was on. The porch was too small for them both to hide without being detected. "Hold on, let me see something." Dee twisted the front door handle to see if it was unlocked. "Damn, it's locked."

"You thought it wouldn't be locked?"

"Yea, people don't lock their doors out here sometimes." Dee started looking under the rug and on top of the door for hiding spots for a spare key.

"What you looking for?"

"A spare key."

Chapter 83

He didn't find a key but when he went to a window, it was a quarter way up. He lifted it up and climbed in from the side of the house and came to the front door to open it for JC.

"Man, you crazy. Let me find out you be breaking into houses and shit," JC said, laughing, walking in. "It stink like dog shit in here. Make sure that nigga ain't got a dog in this bitch." JC started looking around.

Dee, started going through each room, flicking the light on and off. He went upstairs while JC stayed downstairs by the door, looking out the window, waiting for Larry to show up.

As Dee crept up the stairs, he went inside a room and saw a huge dog on the floor sleeping. It didn't have a chain or anything on it. His heart started racing and he thought about closing the door, but he would have to actually take a few more steps and be inside the room to even reach the door handle. "Fuck," he whispered to himself. He crept back down the stairs trying to be as quite as he could. "It's a big ass dog up there sleeping," he whispered.

JC came right over and walked up the stairs not making a noise. Dee was behind him. JC noticed the door and how he could potentially close it but he wasn't about to take the chance. He was thinking the dog wouldn't stop barking if he just shut the door. JC crept closer and Dee stood by the staircase. As JC was getting closer and closer the dog eyes opened and he charged at JC. JC swung the hammer, cracking it right in the head, knocking it completely out cold. He then closed the door. He walked past Dee and didn't say anything. Dee was shocked at how calm JC was about this whole situation. They both sat by the door not saying much, just waiting. They both were texting again.

About two hours later, Larry was pulling in the driveway.

"We got action, "JC said, getting to his feet. Dee stood up as well and grinned.

Larry stumbled up the stairs and was wrestling with his keys. "He drunk I think," Dee whispered as if it wasn't already obvious. As soon as he opened the door, JC clocked him in the head with the hammer.

"Agh shit!" he said as he fell to the ground. JC grabbed him, and yanked him inside the house, closing the door.

Chapter 84

Dee got on top of him, "Remember me?" He started beating him relentlessly with his fist until he was knocked out. JC let him have his way. Dee got up and kicked him all in his face while he was still out cold. JC stood there watching with his arms folded.

Dee kept kicking and stomping him, "Bitch ass nigga!" he said with his last kick to his forehead. Larry's face had swelled up pretty fast, and he looked like he had been in a car accident with all the blood coming from his head.

"You good now?" JC asked, smiling.

"Hell yea," Dee slapped JC hand, letting him know he appreciated him being there. JC walked over to Larry and pulled up the pants he was wearing.

"Go see if it's some money or drugs in this bitch." JC started going through his pockets as well but only found a few dollars. Dee went to search the house and came back empty handed and saw JC on the floor, knocking Larry's kneecap bone loose with the hammer. Dee watched the whole bone break and shift to the side when JC came down on it with the hammer.

"Damn. Bro, what you doing?"

"Making sure this nigga can't walk for a long time, if ever," JC said, as he came down on the other leg hard, waking Larry up. Dee swung and knocked him back out, hitting him in the nose.

JC continued to break as many bones as he could around the kneecaps of Larry. Once he had each leg going a different way, they were out the door, jogging back to the car. JC was in first and saw Dee throwing up outside of the car door before he got in.

"Did you just throw up?"

"Yea."

JC laughed, "You sick nigga?"

"Naw. That shit turned my fucking stomach," he said as he started the car up and drove off. "Why would you break his leg like that?"

Chapter 85

3 weeks later

Akira had been calling and texting JC, sending him pictures of every part of her body. She was wondering where he had been and when he was coming back. Although they were meeting up every so often, it was only for short times. They had met up a couple days ago and had sex in a park, on a baseball bench where he had her screaming about how much she needed him and missed him. That's the day she had told him that her friend was out of the country. She had went to the Dominican Republic to shoot a movie. Now Akira was texting again, wondering when she could see him again.

Akira: JC.

JC: Akira.

Akira: I miss you.

JC: I'm about to call you.

He waited until Roxi went downstairs to chat with her roommates then called her. "Hello."

"You know we can't be texting that kind of shit," JC said, laughing.

"I know, but I delete everything. And Dee don't ever look through my phone. I'm the one that goes through his. Relax, I got this over here JC."

"Ok, ok. What's up? It's about that time, right?"

"For?"

"For you to hold up on your end of the deal."

"She's not even back yet. Can I have a extension please?"

JC laughed. "Come on, an extension? You bet not be playing games with me."

"I swear to God I'm not. I actually called her yesterday, and she's still there in the Dominican Republic. So, you're stuck with me for a second. I can call her on 3 way if you don't believe me."

"Naw you can call her once I get around you."

"Ok, when you going to come back? You over there laid up with your little girlfriend, ignoring me."

"Where Dee at?"

"On the damn game as usual. He in the middle of an international tournament or something."

"Oh, ok ok. You heard from Sara?"

"Um yes. She is looking for your ass. She mad at you. She said you haven't been returning her calls or text."

"All she be wanting to do is fuck. I'm not fucking her no more. Ain't no benefits."

Akira giggled. "Don't do me like that after you meet my friend. I swear I will find you. Do not ghost me."

"I'm not. I'ma need you to stay on my team."

"You better."

JC laughed.

"So, when can I see you?" she asked.

"I'll be over there tomorrow to holla at Dee. And I might stay the night. We will figure something out."

"Ok, well I'll talk to you soon. Did you like my pictures?"

"Hell yea I liked them."

Chapter 86

JC and Roxi watched movies and had sex 3 times before they were asleep. JC tossed and turned all night wondering how long Kelly's people were going to be in Vegas. He also wondered if they thought it was him or not. He was up at about 7a.m showering and brushing his teeth. His hair was growing back and he was planning on letting it grow back long. He called Dee and he was still in the bed, but he told JC he would send Akira to come pick him up. She got up and came right away. Roxi woke up when she felt him kiss her on the cheek.

"You leaving?"

"Yea, I'll see you later. Text me once you get up."

"Ok baby," she said as she kissed him on the lips and hugged him. She watched him walk out to make sure Larry wasn't anywhere hiding again. JC got in the car and drove away.

"Good morning, you up early," Akira said. She still had on slippers, some pajama pants and a t-shirt. She had a messy ponytail straight to the back with some lip gloss on.

"I know, I went to sleep early last night."

"Tired?"

"Yea."

"So, Dee still sleep, I was thinking we can go over my mom's house for a second. They out of town," she said, smiling.

JC smiled, "You just can't get enough huh?"

She giggled, "Not really. So yes?" she asked, winking at him, giving him a sexy look.

"Real quick," he told her, and she headed over there. Her parents' house was about 15 minutes away and they lived in a nice friendly looking neighborhood. She pulled into the garage, opening it with the opener she had inside her car on her sun visor. As they both got out of the car and went inside, she attacked him, kissing him and licking his face.

"I miss you so much," she said, kissing him with her tongue, and ripping his clothes off.

"I miss you too," he said, picking her up as she wrapped her legs around him. "Where we going?"

"Right here, on the couch."

They had sex in the living room for about 30 minutes, but it felt like it lasted 2 hours. Akira loved having sex with him and Dee had become so boring, all she could think about even when they would have sex, was JC. JC liked having sex with her too, but he was more concerned about getting to her friend so he could start making money.

"You got cum dripping all down your leg," he told her as he watched her putting on her shirt.

"Let me wipe this off," she said, as she went to the bathroom giggling.

Chapter 87

Soon they were out the door and heading back to Akira and Dee's house. Once they got back Dee was still sleeping but JC woke him up and he came in talked to him in the living room.

"What's up? I see you den healed up nice."

"Yea man, all that shit went away."

"That's good. So, what's the plan? We gotta start making some moves."

"I can call up them Asian dudes with the weed and see what I can do. I think we can pull it though honestly."

"Well shit, I'm ready. Have your girl, bring this gun to get $4,000 for me," JC whispered.

"Shit I'll do it when I leave out. I have to go take care of some shit in a little while. I know the dude and shit, so he gonna slide me that shit under the table."

"Oh cool. Yea I need that shit. Me and Roxi been spending. We just been laying up, but shit she don't cook, so we eating out, ordering movies and all type of shit. That shit starts to add up," JC said, laughing.

"Man honestly, I need it to. I have a little one on the way. Akira told me she was pregnant the other day, so I have to step my game up and get some money stacked up."

JC stomach turned a little as he was confused for a minute. "Damn."

"Yea man. I'm about to be a father. Shit don't even seem real."

"We will figure something out." JC said before he changed the subject. He was wondering why Akira didn't tell him she was pregnant. Then he wondered if it was his baby or not. All kind of things were running through his head. Everything was happening so fast. Even Roxi had told him she was late coming on her period as well, so he was also waiting to see if she was pregnant too. JC knew he had to make something happen. All this sitting around and having sex for free shit had to come to a halt.

After Dee left, JC was there with Akira and as soon she came out of the room, he confronted her. "Why didn't you tell me you was pregnant? And I thought you was on birth control."

"I was going to. I am on birth control, but it failed."

"Is it a possibility it's mine?"

"I think so."

"Wow. Are you keeping it?"

"I don't believe in abortions."

"So, what if it is mine?"

"I don't know. I'm not going to tell him it's yours."

"So, what you gonna do? Act like it's his?"

"Yes. I don't want to cause any problems. This wasn't supposed to happen like this. But God don't make mistakes."

"You crazy. This some bullshit."

"Why?"

"Because you got me in a fucked up situation now."

"I'm sorry."

Chapter 88

JC shook his head and sat down on the couch and took a deep breath.

"Maybe it's his. Keep a positive mind frame. Don't worry about it too much."

"I hope it is. This shit is crazy."

"He won't blood test the baby, so don't worry. We can do a test on the side. If it's not yours, no problem. If it is, then we will keep it between us only. Simple as that."

"You say that like it's no big deal and that this shit is ok."

"I mean, what can I do? I'm not going to stress about it. You shouldn't neither."

JC thought for a minute. His life was a roller coaster anyway. He thought about all the shit he was up against and then finally made sense of the baby being his, and just said fuck it. It didn't matter. Dee was just a dude he met on the bus. He wasn't his real cousin like they were trying to act like. JC tried to make it better in his head, but he knew he still had created damage. He shouldn't have been having sex with this girl at all.

"Where you been? I thought you was supposed to be staying here. You been staying with the same girl all this time?"

"Yea."

"So you really like her then?"

"Yea, she cool. That's my baby."

"That was fast."

"What was fast?"

"You liking her like that. You guy's just be in the house under each other all day?"

"Shit, all we do is talk and joke all day long. I feel like I've been knowing her for years. We been spending all day together. She's not irritating. We get along good and everything. She don't be all in my business. She's never whining or complaining. So it's cool to be around her. I can't complain."

"Well, that's good. I'm happy for you. I just thought it would have took you longer to meet someone in Vegas that you was actually taking serious."

"Well, I met her on the way to Vegas. So, we had talked so much and bonded just on that long ass bus ride. We clicked right off the bat."

"Aww, how sweet."

Chapter 89

JC could tell there was a little jealousy there, but he felt she didn't have a reason to care about his situation. She had her own thing going on with Dee. This is one of many reasons JC found it hard to trust women.

A few hours later, Dee came back. He had ran some errands for himself and JC. He brought back $4000 for JC for the sale of one of the guns. And he made a few hundred from doing some petty scamming.

"So, the last time I seen these dudes, we met at a house, and it had like 400 pounds in there, all packaged up. Them pounds be going for like $1,600, so you do the math," Dee said.

"Damn. I know they had to have been strapped bro."

"I didn't see one gun present. These Asians like some nerdy dudes. I would be surprised if they even owned a gun."

JC sat and thought about it for a minute. "Let's do a dry run first with some money. If the opportunity there when we get there, we will rob they ass. But let's order like 2 pounds. That's something I can at least pay for."

"Ok that's cool." Dee got on the phone and called them up. He talked to them for about five minutes while they were trying to remember who he was. When they finally managed to identify him, they then sent him an address asking him to meet them at that location. He told him he had a friend in town that was interested in buying a large quantity, but he wanted to see it and test it out first before he did any buying. JC listened closely as Dee talked the details through and then hung up.

As they got ready to head out, they put together all the things they'd need to get them through. They packed a backpack with duct tape, some long rope, and some very strong zip ties. They also had their guns on them just in case things got heated. Akira was trying to be nosey, but Dee had closed the bedroom door on her. JC could hear her walking around, up and down the hallway, trying to get a sense of what was going on. After about ten minutes, she gave up and left, much to JC's relief.

"Man, this our first mission together. Don't be in there freezing up if the shit have to go down," JC told Dee, with a serious look on his face. He wasn't sure how experienced Dee was, and if he was going to freeze up when things started to get dangerous.

"You don't have to worry about that. This ain't my first time, robbing or shooting a nigga. I've did some shit before, plenty of times," Dee told him confidently with a little bit off swagger in his tone.

JC tipped his head, relieved that he wasn't going in with a rookie. "Alright then let's go see what's up."

After they hauled their gear out into the car and secured it in the trunk, they took off. It wasn't too far away from where they were. It took them about 25 minutes to get there, due to traffic. It was a decent neighborhood with nice lawns and well-maintained houses. When they finally found the house they had been instructed to go to, Dee called up the guys and was told to come inside.

"Why you ain't been rob these nigga's?" JC asked, curious as to why Dee was choosing to do this just now.

Dee shrugged and threw a glance at JC. "Shit I don't know. I ain't been hurting for shit, so I wasn't even thinking about shit like that."

Chapter 90

They got out of the car and walked up to the door. It was closed. Dee rang the bell and they waited for a few minutes, but nobody answered the door. He knocked again and an Asian girl answered the door. She was pretty and welcoming. She led them into the house. "Hi, he's in the kitchen. Follow me," she said, smiling and walking away. As they followed her, they both saw Asian guys in every corner as they walked past them. They were holding big guns and not even looking at JC and Dee. When he saw just how many people they were going to have to deal with and how heavily they were armed, JC instantly changed his mind. He knew that he was dealing with some serious people. All the guns and rope they had brought with them wasn't going to be of much use against these guys. They were outnumbered at least ten to one. His heart rate picked up a little as they made it into the kitchen. The kitchen was huge and there were big granite countertops around the whole place. In the middle of the kitchen was a huge table stacked with bags. There were pounds of weed everywhere.

"What's up my guy?" The Asian guy that Dee knew said as he approached him with a friendly grin.

Dee smiled, grabbed his hand and patted him on the back, "What's up? What you got for me?" He asked, trying not to seem nervous. He was a little shaky and JC could tell.

He was afraid that Dee's nervousness might seem off to the Asian guy and that it would get their guard up. The last thing he wanted to do was get all the guys in the house suspicious. "This my cousin JC. This the one that wanted to see some shit," Dee explained.

"What's up, JC? Where you from, buddy?" the Asian guy asked.

"Michigan."

"Detroit?"

"Yes sir." JC gave him the most genuine grin he could muster.

"Hell yea man. I've been out there a few years back. When I went it was cold as hell man, and I didn't bring a damn coat. I had on this thin ass jacket," he said, laughing and making the four other guys that were in the kitchen with him laugh right along too. They all had guns. JC looked at the guns and then turned to the guy who had been talking to him.

"What's up with all the guns?" JC asked, nodding at the weapons in the men's hands.

"Protection. It's crazy out here. Got to have protection."

"Oh ok. I didn't know Vegas was that dangerous."

"Well, it's not. But sometimes, things can get dangerous, if you know what I mean." JC could tell that the guy wasn't kidding.

"I stay away from danger. But I get it."

"So, what you looking for?" he asked, looking at JC and then at Dee.

"I'm looking for some shit that's a good price and it smoke good as well. I was hoping to look at a few different kinds, then maybe take a sample back to my homeboys that I brought out here with me and let them tell me what they think."

"I'll give you some samples. No problem. Check these out."

The guy stood up and went over to a kitchen cabinet to pull out a box filled to the brim.

Chapter 91

He showed JC a few different kinds and explained a few things about them too. JC played his role like they had planned, smelling it and breaking each bud apart. "This one nice," he said, holding up a bud. "How much for a pound of this?"

"I can do those for $1400."

"What if I get 50 to a 100?" JC watched the guy closely to see his reaction to what he would think was a big deal.

The Asian guy's eye brows raised and he sat straighter in his chair, realizing that this was starting to look like some real heavy business. "Oh, you trying to really buy some weight? If you buy a hundred, I'll do $100,000. How long does it take you to get rid of 100 pounds?"

"If it's good, no longer than a week." JC sat back and stretched a little.

"All in Detroit?"

"Yep."

Dee listened as they were talking. So far, JC had been doing most of the talking and all he had to do was play along. He was still nervous, but JC was breaking the ice just fine. He had came off pretty friendly to them so things were going along pretty smoothly. He had set his bag down and walked away from it. Dee listened as JC told a whole story about what he had going on in Michigan and how much weed he could move.

"So, take this, take some of that and take this one. Let them smoke that. And if they like it, let's do some business."

The guy handed JC three different kinds. It was about 3 grams of each one. "Ok cool. Do you deliver?"

"Eventually. First, we have to do a couple transactions then we can work something out, cool?"

"Yea that's cool."

"So let me know what they think, and we will set something up."

"Cool," JC said, nodding in agreement.

"Thanks man. I appreciate this. I'll let you know something soon." They all slapped hands and Dee and JC left the house. They quickly jumped in the car. "Man, sorry about that shit. They ain't never had guns when I came around," Dee explained, still a little shaken by what they had seen inside.

"Man, soon as I walked in, I was ready to go," JC huffed. "They looked like they was waiting on some shit to pop off. I didn't like that shit at all."

"My bad."

"It's all good, you ain't know," JC mumbled. Dee nodded, relieved that things were alright.

"Man, we might as well hit the strip club tonight and see what we can catch."

"What you mean?" JC was curious as to what Dee was going on about. "What do you mean catch?"

Dee laughed. "Nigga, them strippers be having money. We can follow and rob one of them."

Chapter 92

JC was quiet for a second. He was thinking. It seemed like an easy enough way to score some cash, but there had to be a way to get more than whatever the strippers had on them. "They all got pimps too, right?" he asked.

"Yea, most of them," Dee agreed.

"Fuck robbing the stripper. Let's get the pimp."

Dee shrugged. "I'm down with that too. It's whatever."

As they were on their way home, Dee was on his phone texting and barely paying attention to the road. His hands were just lightly grazing the wheel as his fingers flew over the screen of his phone. When he avoided a head on collision by a hair, JC spoke up. "Damn nigga, you swerving and shit."

"My bad," Dee said, as he got back in his lane and started texting again. "I'ma drop you off at the crib for about a hour. I have to go take care of something."

"Alright that's cool."

"Or you want to go to Roxi's until I finish?"

"Naw, she ain't gone want a nigga to leave back out. I'll see her ass later."

They both started laughing.

"Akira there, and if you need to go anywhere, just let her know."

"Ok cool."

They pulled up at Dee's place and they both went into the house. They were greeted by Akira who seemed very happy to see Dee. Dee went inside the room with Akira while JC sat on the couch, turning on the video game. He sat his bag down right next to him to keep it safe. He wanted to take all the stuff out but didn't want Akira to come out and see. After a few minutes passed by and Akira was nowhere to be seen, he just grabbed a few things out and closed it back. Soon, Dee came out the room. "I'll see you in a little while."

"Alright, bet," JC responded.

"Heyy JC, how you doing?" Akira asked as she walked Dee to the door. They kissed before she closed the door behind him.

"I'm good. How you doing?"

"I'm good," she said, as she walked to the kitchen. She was wearing some purple spandex shorts with two white stripes on each side of the leg. Her round booty stuck out as JC watched her walk. She had a nice firm ass with just the right amount of jiggle to it and it was hard to keep his eyes off her when she was walking around like that.

"What you been up to?" He asked as he watched her. She came out of the kitchen with a glass of water in her hand.

"Nothing much. Mad I can't drink because of this pregnancy," she said with a little attitude.

"Oh yeah, you on restriction," he said with a short laugh.

"Yes. It sucks too."

"You'll be alright."

"Come here," she said, as she walked to the room using her index finger, telling him to follow her in.

"You tripping," he said, smiling, shaking his head. He couldn't believe she was really coming on to him at this moment. Maybe it was the pregnancy hormones or something making her horny.

"How? He's not going to be coming back for a while." She smiled a sultry smile at him.

"I know, but let's leave or something. I ain't feeling it right now, just fucking in the crib like this," he told her.

She walked to the door and locked the dead bolt on the door. She turned to look at him, her hands on her hips. "He couldn't even get in if he wanted to, JC."

He shook his head. "I don't feel like it, Akira."

"Just come in here. I'll make you feel like it," she said as she stood by the door to the bedroom. She looked succulent and gorgeous, all radiant and juicy with the pregnancy hormones but he ignored her and kept playing his video game.

JC's attention was still on the game until she came and straddled his lap, and started kissing him. "Why you acting like that?" she said as she stopped kissing him for a second. She sounded a little hurt that he was ignoring her.

"Because."

She kissed him again, her lips puckering against his, "Because what?" she asked, now feeling his dick hardening through his pants. "He seems to want it." She giggled.

JC laughed and she was kissing him again. They tongue wrestled for a couple minutes, while he was rubbing on her soft booty. This girl was so sexy, and she knew it. JC could tell she knew she could have him any time she wanted him. He couldn't understand why Dee was not always all over her.

JC felt the wetness through her shorts from her pussy. It was seeping through. "Damn, that pussy wet as hell," he said, as he continued to kiss her.

"Look at what you did baby," she murmured as she kept kissing him and slightly humping him, grinding on his lap in a slow rhythm that drove him crazy. "Just put it in, baby," she moaned, now licking and kissing on his neck and ears.

Chapter 93

He soon picked her up, walked her to the bedroom and laid her down on the bed. "No, you lay down," she told him as she got up and pushed him back on the bed. She pulled his pants and underwear halfway down to his knees and then noticed the gun that was tucked in his waistband. "Why you have this gun on you?"

"My bad," he said, putting the gun away on the side table. They started kissing again and she moved lower, putting his dick in her mouth and started sucking on it. It didn't matter what time of the day it was, Akira always wanted to have sex with JC. She loved the way he made her body feel and she wanted more of him. She was greedy for his dick.

JC just laid back and enjoyed every second of it. He was enjoying himself, but he couldn't stop thinking about certain things in his life. He had a lot on his mind. Akira was pregnant, Roxi was a few days late on her period and could possibly be pregnant as well. Juicy was also pregnant and he was wanted for murder. He had to make some money fast and change his identity. Otherwise, he risked getting found and caught, then he'd go away for a long time. He thought about going back to Michigan where he knew he could for sure get some money. He knew way more people out there, plus he knew how to move there. It was more challenging to get started on things in a city that was completely new to him.

Akira climbed on top of him and sat slowly on his dick until it filled her up to the max. "It always feels so good," she whispered as she worked his dick towards the right spot inside her. He held on to her ass cheeks as she did her thing. She looked him in his eyes as her face squinted from the pleasure and pain.

JC soon heard a noise, like someone was coming through the door. "Oh shit!" Akira whispered, as she heard the noise too. "Dee's back!" she exclaimed, rolling over and rushing to put her shorts back on. She started fixing her hair and making sure everything was good. There was loud knocks coming from the door and she rushed out of the bedroom. "Who is it!" she yelled.

JC was grabbing his gun and while he was pulling his briefs up, the door was being kicked in. They came in so fast, that JC's eyes grew big when he noticed Nino, Dee and two other guys who were dressed in all black. They had knocked the door off the hinges, and JC wasn't sure if there were more of them coming behind them or not. Akira screamed as she displayed a confused look on her face. She was scared from seeing all the guns that were pointing at them and embarrassed at the same time...

Other books by the A. Roy Milligan

Women Lie Men Lie part 1

Women Lie Men Lie part 2

Women Lie Men Lie part 3

Women Lie Men Lie part 5 coming soon

Stack Before Your Splurge

Naive To The Streets

Girls Fall Like Dominoes

Fifty Shades Of Snow

Fifty Shades Of Snow part 2

Fifty Shades Of Snow part 3

Self-help books:

From Prison To The Car Hauling Game

From Prison To The Publishing Game

Please, please please, leave a review.

https://www.amazon.com/A-Roy-Milligan/e/B009YEVZPC?ref=sr_ntt_srch_lnk_2&qid=1587560927&sr=8-2